GRACE

Also by Chika Unigwe

The Phoenix
On Black Sisters' Street
Night Dancer
The Middle Daughter

GRACE

CHIKA UNIGWE

CANONGATE

First published in Great Britain in 2026
by Canongate Books Ltd, 14 High Street, Edinburgh EH1 1TE

canongate.co.uk

1

Copyright © Chika Unigwe, 2026

The right of Chika Unigwe to be identified as the
author of this work has been asserted by her in accordance
with the Copyright, Designs and Patents Act 1988

No part of this book may be used or reproduced in any manner for the purpose of
training artificial intelligence technologies or systems. This work is reserved from
text and data mining (Article 4(3) Directive (EU) 2019/790)

British Library Cataloguing-in-Publication Data
A catalogue record for this book is available on
request from the British Library

ISBN 978 1 83726 192 5

Typeset in Bembo by Palimpsest Book Production Ltd,
Falkirk, Stirlingshire

Printed and bound by CPI Group (UK) Ltd, Croydon CR0 4YY

The manufacturer's authorised representative in the EU for product safety is
Authorised Rep Compliance Ltd, 71 Lower Baggot Street, Dublin D02 P593
Ireland (arccompliance.com)

For Stef, Ral, Tomike and Jefeechi: my miracles. I may not always be the mother you want, but I'll always be the one that you need

PART ONE

One

New Lay Out, Enugu

2020

The cake looked disturbingly like mud. It tasted nothing of the Chocolatey Goodness it was called, but Grace ploughed on. Digging into it, bringing fork to mouth, determined to repeat the motion until her stomach revolted. Each forkful a penance, bitter on her tongue. Tears stung her eyes and inside bellowed a scream she could not let out. There wasn't much left to the six-inch cake she had bought in anticipation of today. The family, used to treats appearing randomly in the fridge, hadn't questioned her about buying such an elaborately decorated cake. Buttercream swirls piped all around it. No one else seemed interested because, unlike the doughnuts she'd bought from the same baker, the cake was still untouched when Grace had brought it out this morning. She sat at the kitchen table that Cee, the family's domestic help, used as a chopping board. Grace imagined herself exploding, bits and pieces of her splattering all over the wood, her blood seeping into the grooves. Soon, the rest of the house would begin to awaken. Okika first, and then their teenage twins, Kaikele and Mmuodum. Okika would not think it odd that she was already up, and the twins expected that the way of the world was that parents always woke first. None of them would note that the day was anything but ordinary. Grace preferred it that way. Apart from the cake, she kept no other rituals. How would she begin to explain to this family she had created, the family she nurtured, the family without whom she was nothing, about the secret she buried inside her like a seed in deep soil, hoping that her own willpower would be enough to keep it from sprouting? Not a single one of them would understand. If there was anything Grace's life had taught her, it was that love wasn't a given. It could be taken away. Once she was no longer the person they thought they knew, their feelings too would change. It had happened before, in her previous life. She took another forkful of cake. Her cheeks bulged like a squirrel's. The food burned her throat but Grace would not give up.

Every year, she did this; she ate a cake on Baby's birthday. At the beginning, it had been those horrible triangular-shaped travesties made with palm oil rather than butter that she had bought with money pilfered from her father's shirt pocket or her mother's purse. She would tear open the plastic wrapping of the cake even before leaving the store and would always eat all of it before going home. Later, when she could, she began buying better cakes, cakes with icing that melted in her mouth, but burned all the way to her stomach, settled like mixed cement. Grace was not superstitious, but she believed in *things*. Like this ritual for one. Wherever Baby was, it connected Grace to her. If she gave it up, if she missed one year, then Baby would become a ghost.

Nobody else knew of Baby. Not her husband, not her children, not her best friend, Ifeatu, who imagined that she knew everything there was to know about Grace. If her secret made it out, made it to BellaNaija or Linda Ikeji or one of the other gossip blogs, she'd lose everything. She was a deacon in the church, a well-respected business owner, a decorated midwife. OFR. Order of the Federal Republic of Nigeria. And one day, she hoped to run for political office. She would start with a senate seat, cut her teeth there. With the right support, she could pull it off. She already knew what her campaign slogan would be: For One and All. She would have photos of herself surrounded by babies, two of whom would be in her arms. To have a successful shot, she needed to not just have money, she also had to be perfect. The world did not forgive women it found wanting. She could not afford a scandal. Everything she'd worked for would crumble if her secret came out, and she could not – would not – have that. She poured out a cup of coffee. Black. No sugar. The way she had learned to drink it when she began to shed other parts of her old self to replace them with a new persona so that she could live. She grazed her fork against the piece of cake on her plate. A more attentive husband might have noticed after fifteen years of being with her that her mood swings and the cake eating always happened on the same date each year. The fourth of June. But not Okika. Grace was not complaining. A more attentive husband would have made her life more difficult with all his questions and she might not have been able to keep her secret this long. There were times she thought that that was why she had married Okika. He was a good husband, a good man, but even good men had their limits. She raised a hand, heavy with melancholy, and took another bite of the cake.

During the compulsory marriage counselling class they had taken before their wedding, Grace and Okika had been cautioned to be truthful about everything. Lay your secrets bare to each other, the priest said. The sort of thing a person who had never been in a relationship would say, Grace thought. Everybody else knew that the key to a happy relationship, especially marriage, lay in holding your secrets within your fist and making sure you didn't loosen your grasp. She didn't want to know everything about Okika. She knew enough and that would do. At the beginning of their relationship, Okika had told her he had a child with an ex-girlfriend in the US. He didn't want her finding out from anybody else. 'I'm not really in his life but I just thought, you know, that you should know.' She said *Okay, thanks for telling me,* like it was nothing, but she had spent days marvelling at how easy it had been for him to say it. He had offered the information with no trepidation, no sense that it had the potential to torpedo his life, just said it with the same casualness with which he had told her of the car he had before they met, slipping it in between ordering lunch at Madam Volvo's and switching off his phone, which had begun to vibrate. The ex was American. Sophia. They had met at the University of Georgia. She had fallen pregnant, decided to keep the baby. She didn't ask him what he wanted, didn't ask him to marry her like a Nigerian would have, he said. 'Besides, I was young, was in no state to marry anyone or raise a kid, so that was good.' He graduated when the baby was just under a year old and returned to Nigeria. 'She didn't do long distance, moving to Nigeria wasn't an option for her and the breakup was amicable.' Did he miss his child? Grace asked. Okika paused, mid chew, tapped his spoon against the plate in front of him and said, 'No. I mean, I don't really know him. Sophia used to send me pictures until he started elementary school. Maybe she got tired of sending them. But everyone in my life knows of him, just in case he comes back one day when he's old enough, looking for me.' Would you want him to? Grace had asked. 'I guess. I mean, he's mine. It'd be nice if he did, but it's got to be his choice.' That boy would be twenty-eight now, two years older than Baby.

Grace scooped up another piece of cake, shovelled it into her mouth and swallowed without tasting. It formed a lump in her throat which she chased down with coffee. There were times she thought of Okika's baby, of the ex that had been able to make such a choice even though she was only nineteen at the time. This American ex that hadn't worried about what people would say. But always, Grace's thoughts were on Baby. She wiped the tears that had begun to roll down her face. She thought of Ben, and a curse escaped her lips. She hoped that, wherever he was, he was suffering as much as she was. Outside, the rest of the neighbourhood was waking up. When their house was being built, Grace had insisted on a kitchen that looked out onto the compound. She couldn't remember why now, but it meant that from the kitchen one heard the world. Laughter spilled into her ears from beyond the walled fence surrounding the house. Grace envied the easy laughter. For twenty-six years, she had not laughed like that. There was always sadness trimming the edges of her laughter so that she couldn't completely immerse herself in it. She wiped her eyes, her hands heavy with grief. The itinerant preacher who patrolled the neighbourhood punctually between six and seven-thirty every morning tinkled his bell. That was her cue. She too would have to get ready for work. She pushed the chair away from the table and stood. Her legs felt wobbly as if she was drunk, and for a second she thought she would fall. She held onto the table, shut her eyes and inhaled. Today, she would rather be anywhere else but at the clinic, surrounded by posters of babies with fat cheeks and happy laughter. She exhaled and opened her eyes. The preacher's bell continued, insistent and urgent, as Grace staggered her way back into the bedroom she shared with Okika.

Two

New Haven, Enugu

1993

At New Haven Secondary School, NHSS, the bell rang for assembly at seven-thirty every morning. Any student who missed it, even by a minute, was punished. The punishment was arbitrary depending on the mood of the principal – from not being allowed on the playground during recess to being caned on the buttocks – and Grace tried her best to avoid it. However, one Tuesday morning in January, she was late out of bed and therefore late to school. She was rounded up with about a dozen other latecomers and handed machetes to clear the grass sprouting outside the principal's house. One of the other dozen students was Ben. A year ahead of Grace at school, he was tall and spindly. Wildly popular and fashionable, his crewcut hair style always oiled, he looked like Will Smith from *The Fresh Prince of Bel Air*. He and Grace moved in different circles, although what Grace had could hardly be called a circle: two girls in her class with whom she sometimes hung out during recess. Students like herself from modest homes, made timid by their polyester schoolbags and rubber sandals, they stayed away from the wealthier students whose parents could afford private schools if they chose to. There was nothing to distinguish Grace, nothing to make her visible to the likes of Ben. But Ben had sought her out, of all the other students who were serving punishment that morning. He had chosen a spot near her and started a conversation. At first, she hadn't been sure he was talking to her. When she asked, 'Are you talking to me?' he'd laughed and said, 'I'm not sure. Am I?' His eyes danced with mischief behind his glasses. Grace laughed too, although she didn't think it was funny. Her stomach fluttered as if a thousand butterflies were flapping around inside. Her palms felt sweaty and her grip on her machete loosened so much that she almost dropped it.

The world of NHSS was split sharply in two: the popular students, aka the *happening* students, and the others. Sometimes the two orbits collided and something magical happened. Or that was how it seemed to Grace when Ben, the shiniest star in the *happening* orbit, asked her to be his girlfriend six days later, on a Monday morning after assembly, his glasses sparkling with light, hands in the pockets of his bright blue school trousers. How could she say no? At NHSS, that was all it took to date: someone asked you to be their boyfriend or girlfriend. You said yes or no as you desired. Grace said yes to Ben because she liked him, because she liked his tall, skinny frame, because she wanted to know what it was like to be kissed by him. To belong with the *happening* students. And she was curious about other things too, especially the things her mother would never talk to her about. Once, she asked her mother how babies were made. 'A man marries a woman; they pray and ask God for a baby, and it happens.'

Grace was twelve years old then and had just witnessed a neighbour's dog jump on the back of another dog, had watched an older neighbour throw a stick at the dogs to separate them and mutter something about how it was no wonder the female dog kept giving birth every few months. Grace knew that babies didn't happen because people prayed. She wanted to know how a dog on the back of another dog translated to babies and if it was the same for humans, although she could not imagine how her father on the back of her mother could have resulted in something as real, as solid as her. She sulked out of her mother's room, dawdled outside the bathroom door where her father was shaving and decided against asking him. She could not imagine that he – who never said much anyway – would give her an answer that was any more sensible than her mother's. Grown-ups could be so annoying. Now she was fifteen, she knew a bit more (thanks to the Integrated Science and Biology classes she had taken since then and conversations with her more mature classmates) and she wondered if the stories she heard, of an enjoyment so intense you forgot yourself, were true.

Grace and Ben became a 'thing', inseparable at school, walking home together, the willowy Ben hanging off her sturdier frame like an appendage, giggling all the way until they turned into Grace's street where an adult might see them and report back to Grace's parents, and then she would be in trouble. Ben, older by one year, brought her gifts of biscuits and sausage rolls from his parents' supermarket, and occasionally half-full bottles of perfume pilfered from his mother's room. Earrings and bangles she hid from her parents but showed off at school, shaking her wrists so that the bracelets jingled. They spent recess together, hiding behind the toilet block to exchange chewing-gum-flavoured kisses that seemed to end far too quickly for Grace.

It felt to Grace as if Ben's shine had rubbed off on her. She was still the quiet student with no friends – except for the two girls in her class – but now she glowed, and even senior students said hello to her. Three weeks after they began to date, Ben invited her to a party at one of his friends'. Another senior student whose uncle was a commissioner, and who could already drive. It was a night party and Grace knew that there was no excuse she could come up with that would make her parents allow her to leave the house that late. 'How can I go to a party without my girlfriend? Am I dating a baby?' Ben asked. For the first time, Grace worried that her happiness would not last, that Ben would find someone else. A *happening* female student. One of those who knew how to sneak out to parties, like Patience in his class. Patience went to night parties, sneaking out after her parents were in bed and sneaking back in before they woke up. Once, when Grace was with Ben and his group of friends during recess, Patience had told them of how she had to bribe one of her numerous sisters to cover for her should any problems arise. 'So far, so good,' she said and winked at Grace. Patience and her boyfriend had broken up. What if Ben asked her out instead?

Three

New Lay Out, Enugu

2020

Grace felt that there were moments in her life when her happiness seemed almost complete. But was it still happiness if something was missing? Isn't happiness like a pregnancy? You either are or you aren't? What was it her classmate in elementary school used to say? Nearly cannot kill a bird but fechala its odu. A bird that's nearly killed by a pebble from a catapult grazing its feathers is still a bird that is alive. As long as she did not dwell on it, Grace could convince herself that she was happy, that what was missing did not affect this. Now was one of those moments as she watched the twins and Okika playing WHOT, their laughter ringing through the house. 'Go to the market!' Kaikele shouted, her voice rising gleefully with triumph. She flung a card on top of the rising pile in the centre of the table. Both Mmuodum and Okika picked a card from the deck. Kaikele placed another card and said, 'Continue.'

'Pick two!' Mmuodum added, slapping a card onto the table. It landed with a sharp thwap, sending the neat stack in the centre trembling. She gave her sister a high five.

Okika groaned dramatically, his shoulders slumping in exaggerated defeat. 'Ah ah! You children want to finish me today! No mercy for your father,' he cried, his voice half-laughing, half-despairing, as he reached toward the pile. He picked up two cards with deliberate reluctance, groaning as if the weight of the cards was suddenly too much to bear. 'Pick another two,' Mmuodum shouted, and applauded herself. Okika picked two more and dropped his head theatrically on the table. The girls erupted into fresh laughter, their heads thrown back, shoulders touching as they leaned into each other. They were already gloating at their father's impending loss.

Grace watched them, her daughters – radiant with life, their smooth, bright skin incandescent in the afternoon light filtering through the curtains – and their father, teasing each other as they played. She thought again how relentless her children's joy was. At their age, she was no longer a child. She had had to grow up quickly, and yet, she had once had a happy childhood. Sunday afternoons like this, playing games with her parents. Ludo. Nchorokoto. AJAQ. She remembered her father trying to teach her draughts and her mother teasing him that he was teaching their daughter the 'game for beer drinkers. What's next? You'll take her to Mama Nnewi's for ugba and Guinness?' She had once laughed as unrestrained as her children. Her eyes misted. She walked past the table, towards the kitchen.

'Mommy, come and play,' Mmuodum called out.

Grace paused. She wanted to say yes. She always wanted to say yes. But something – maybe that ache that rose in her whenever she watched them play, maybe the fear that she would cry and spill it all – always held her back. It felt to her that she was always standing at the margins of this family she had co-created, too scared to look into its shiny, sunny centre lest she be burned.

'Maybe later,' she said, forcing her voice to behave, forcing it not to betray the pain she carried. She rarely joined in their games. She told them she preferred to watch. 'Someone has to be a supporter abi?' But deep down, she knew the truth.

She opened the kitchen door and shut it behind her. She needed a moment – just a moment – to gather herself, to soften the edges of the memories roiling inside her, and then she would go and sit at the table and watch this family she had manifested be joyful. She opened the fridge and took out a Tupperware with leftover jollof. She grabbed a spoon and began to eat it cold to push down the quiet grief that was scrambling to let out. Her chest hurt from swallowing the rice too quickly so that she didn't have to taste how awful cold rice was. From the dining room, the sounds of Okika and the girls streamed in. Now, they were playing another game, and Okika was begging for mercy. This was their Sunday after-lunch routine. Family time, Grace called it. They played games, they gorged on Nollywood, they danced. Right from when the twins were toddlers, Grace had been intentional in carving out 'family time.' There were days, like today, when it seemed to her that she'd wanted it as proof that she had a family, that they were a unit, a complete unit. And if they were that, then nothing could be missing. Days like today it became altogether too much for her and she had to fight to hold back tears. She took a deep breath, dumped the now empty container in the sink and counted to ten. She tried not to think of Baby. She especially tried not to think of Ben.

Four

New Lay Out, Enugu

2020

Of all the dreams that Grace had had, running a baby factory was not one of them. The term used to have her thinking of concrete buildings and machines spewing out body parts: torsos in one bin, heads and limbs in another. And even when she got to know better, when she learned that they weren't all holding houses for abducted women forced to get pregnant so that their babies could be sold, that some were orphanages and clinics providing services that they believed were necessary, she still wanted no part of it. Yet like almost everything else in her life, that she would pivot into running one had blindsided her. The choice had been made for her ten years ago when a woman had walked into her maternity clinic, sweaty and frantic. The clinic wasn't much at the time, a three-room ward and an office. It was just Grace and a retired nurse who worked part time, coming in only when Grace needed a hand. Grace walked the woman through into her office, a small space with room enough for just a table and three chairs. She thought she could guess what this woman wanted; she was used to it. Women who came to her this late in their pregnancies often couldn't afford the exorbitant fees of the bigger private clinics, but, wanting the same level of care, they came to her hoping for government-hospital rates. Mostly these women came with their husbands, and once they heard her rates – hers was a small clinic but she treated each patient like a VIP – they begged for such ridiculous discounts or stretched-out payment plans that Grace had once burst into laughter. It was a rarity that a woman ever came alone. Tall and skinny, the pregnancy looked out of place on this one. It was as if someone had tied a bundle over the woman's stomach to feign a pregnancy. She was not young – she looked on the wrong side of forty – so probably not a first-time mother. Once any patient walked into her office, Grace began what she termed her 'judgement call'. She guessed their circumstances before they had even said a word. She took in how they dressed, how they carried themselves, what social class they belonged to. It helped her prepare for a firm and unequivocal response. If she gave everyone discounts, she wouldn't be able to repay the bank loan she had taken to set up the clinic. She could not afford to run a charity, or she would be back at the poorly funded government hospital where they were always owed salaries. Staying home and doing nothing, allowing Okika to look after her, would kill her. She had sworn a long time ago that she would not be that wife who asked for housekeeping money and money to do her hair and nails. It would crush her to be reduced to that. This woman, she decided, could afford her.

'I cannot keep this baby, please. Dash it to somebody else,' the woman said even before she sat, stunning Grace out of her thoughts. The gold watch on her wrist glittered.

Her eyes, too small for her face, didn't blink as she held Grace's gaze. Most people spilled out of the narrow plastic chair Grace had in her office in those days, but not this woman, who fit perfectly into it, sitting upright. There was something about her that transcended mere beauty and made Grace imagine that she was used to getting her way. Grace admired her forthrightness and was intrigued. In this country, people prevaricated, especially if they were requesting a favour, starting with all sorts of mundane questions – *How's the family? How're the children?* – before landing on the reason for their visit. This forthrightness was refreshing but it didn't help Grace. She still wasn't sure what the woman wanted from her, but she knew that the woman wouldn't give up easily, whatever it was she was after. She reminded Grace of the popular girls at her secondary school, the way they carried themselves with the easy confidence of the admired, the followership they commanded. No, the followership they *expected*. She waited for the woman to speak. Maturity had taught Grace to allow for silence. There were no patients she had to see. At the moment, her only patient hadn't dilated enough for delivery to be imminent, and so Grace had sent her home. So yes, Grace had time. The woman wore a short, silky, bobbed wig. Grace was sure it was the more expensive human hair type. 'I'm a widow. I got pregnant before my husband died. My in-laws . . .' She stopped. She had switched to Igbo. Her dialect was distinct, replacing all the 'F' sounds with 'V'. 'Va choo ka m . . .' She paused again, hissed, and shook her head as if the words would not come forth. Grace knew all about how widows were treated by certain in-laws. Dead husbands' brothers, especially if they were poor, turning up and stripping the widow of everything her husband owned. It was a common story, so common that not even Nollywood could find ways to make it original.

'My husband's brother wants to marry me,' she said finally. 'That's the only way I am allowed to stay in the house with my children. I have five already. I can't take care of a new one. I can't work if I have a baby. And I don't want to marry my husband's brother. I can't.' She snapped her fingers over her head in disgust. 'The man stinks like a fish. I'd rather die than have him touch me. And he has his own family he's barely looking after. He only wants his hands on his brother's house.' She stopped as if waiting for a response from Grace. Grace said nothing. She wondered what sort of job the woman did. She sounded educated, and while not wealthy enough to move out of the house that had belonged to her and her husband (which would free her from his brother), she could obviously raise five children on her own without their help, and seemed able to withstand the strong current of their animosity. So far. Time was running out for her, clearly. But how could she, Grace, help? The air-conditioning unit behind Grace dripped water into a bucket, its *plop plop plop* of water the only sound in the room. Finally, the woman spoke again. 'I have nothing. O nwero ive m nwe. I can't afford the baby. Please, help me. Find it a home.' The woman steepled her hands under her chin. Grace noticed now that the watch on the woman's wrist, which she had mistaken for gold, was too shiny to be real. It was probably some cheap piece from the market. Now that she looked at the wig properly, it had the tangled look of an old synthetic wig. The woman's hand fluttered, but she didn't say anything else. Grace understood the helplessness of carrying a pregnancy that you hadn't planned for. She felt a tightness in her chest. If she kept the baby, the woman said, she would not be able to escape this greedy brother-in-law. She could leave with her five children and try to save them all. It would be hard, but it was possible. With an infant, it would be impossible. Grace looked at the woman before her who seemed to be trying very hard not to cry. The woman looked back at Grace. Her voice fell, as if she were praying. 'Sister, my life is in your hands. I went to the Motherless Babies and the director chased me out. What type of a witch was I, she asked, that I would want to give up my own child?' She hissed, and for a while neither woman said anything. The woman let out a short, bitter cackle. 'The useless woman asked me to go and marry my husband's brother. Can you imagine it?' Grace *could* imagine it. She could imagine not being allowed to have any options. She tried not to think of that night in 1994. It was difficult because she could think of nothing else in that moment. She had never stopped thinking about it; it was a part of her. Without that night, she could have been living a different life. She didn't regret Okika and her twins, didn't regret this clinic she now had, or the path she had taken to it, but she did wonder, sometimes, who she would have been had it not been for Baby. And what she was forced to do after having Baby. That night had always haunted her. 'I am not sure what I can do,' Grace said.

'I'll kill myself,' the woman said, a steely determination in her voice. 'I'll kill myself rather than live with *that* man.' Maybe it was the determination in her voice, the fierceness in it, or maybe she wanted to right some wrong in the world. Maybe it was the thought of Baby and the options she herself hadn't had, but Grace found herself agreeing to help. She asked the woman to come back in three days, settling on three because she considered it a lucky number, one of the *things* Grace believed in despite not being superstitious. If anyone had asked her, and Grace was being truthful, she would have told them that she had no idea at all of how she could help. Being precise, landing on three days fortified her, it assured her that she'd find a way. And as Grace drove home that evening, the thought slithered into her mind like a worm. She knew a woman from her Christian Women's Association who had been married seven years. The woman had always wanted to adopt, but her husband would not agree. He wanted them to have 'their own'. He wanted his own blood. 'How long does he want to keep trying?' the woman said to Grace one day as they chatted after a meeting, standing in the car park. 'Have you gone for tests? Figured out what's wrong?' Grace asked. The woman gave her a short, sad smile. 'You know, he won't even have his sperm tested. I read up on it, motility and the rest. He says he doesn't fire blanks. As for me, everything is in order. I am sure the problem is his, but what can I do?' Suddenly, it seemed as if the woman realized that she had said too much, hanging out her family's dirty laundry. She told Grace she had to go and jumped into her car.

Now, not even two hours since the widow had left her clinic holding on to the sliver of hope Grace had given her, Grace fumbled in her bag for her phone. Her hands shook as she tapped in the woman's number. She didn't know if this would work, but this was the only option she had. If she worded it well, if she said all the right things, she just might be able to help two families. It turned out that the woman from her Christian Women's Association could persuade her husband to let them 'adopt' if it was not really an adoption. If Grace could make out the birth certificate in their name, they would be delighted to take the child. If she had to eat a toad, Grace said to Okika later that night, it had to be a fat one. Grace billed them N250,000. She knew they were wealthy enough to afford it. Two days later, when the widow returned to her clinic, Grace could tell her that there were ready parents for the baby. She had expected the woman to ask questions, but the woman shook her head. She said a quiet thank you. When she stood to leave, her shoulders seemed hunched. She reminded Grace of something being squeezed into a too-small container. Once the widow went into labour and came to the clinic, Grace called the new parents so that they could be there to hear the healthy cry from the lungs of their first child. Grace could no longer remember if the widow ever touched the baby or if she preferred not to, as some of the women did, because it made it easier to hand over the babies, but Grace remembered that the woman cried when Grace gave her a check for N200,000 to help her set up a business and keep her husband's brother away from her. It could also have been, Grace thought now, that the woman was crying for the baby she sacrificed so that the siblings could live.

 The tiny seed planted that day multiplied and grew, spreading tenaciously like weed. Now, she had the Governor's number on WhatsApp. Her name had been floated at the beginning of this Governor's tenure as his Commissioner for Gender and Women's Affairs but she wasn't interested. She had her sights set higher. At the moment, she was happy to stay out of politics. She could not serve both the government and her own private business. She and the Chief of Police were on a first-name basis. In her line of work, she learned early on, it paid to be friends with the right people. Things got murkier if you yourself were part of the centre of power, if you were seen to align yourself with a particular party, play favourites. Proximity to power was all that was needed. But not close enough as to get burned. So, every year, at Christmas and on Independence Day, she sent hampers of goodies to all the right people in her network, regardless of their political affiliations. She kept her business and herself free of scandals. She donated money to her church and to local schools; she gave interviews and talks in schools, encouraging young people to consider midwifery: 'A noble, worthy vocation. Where would the world be without midwives?' Yet Grace had not always wanted to be a midwife, never mind what she said in all the interviews. 'You know, my own mother was a midwife too, so you could say it runs in the blood.' She had said this so often, created an image of a mother to whom she looked up and after whom she modelled herself, that there were times she caught herself believing it. The same way she believed the other things she said, all the lies she had to construct and keep carefully guarded if the life she had now was not to fall apart. But, she asked herself, were they still lies if she believed them?

After she finished secondary school, barely passing her exams, Grace had sat at home for a year doing nothing. Her life had hit an obstacle she could not cross. She was out of touch with the few friends she had had at the school, and the ones she shared with Ben avoided her like the plague once they broke up. After Grace and her parents moved, she had not made any new ones. She sat herself in front of the TV every day, watching whatever ABS or NTA had on offer while gorging on soaked yellow gari and groundnuts. She rarely paid attention to the programmes. Neither of the two stations offered anything substantial anyway. But Grace liked to fill the house with voices so that she did not have to hear the one in her head calling her worthless. Stupid. Wicked. Baby Killer. On one such day, her father, who had taken to mostly ignoring her, said, 'You need to do something. Repeat SS3 and take JAMB so you can go to the university.' He turned off the TV and stood in front of it.

'I don't want to go.' Grace didn't raise her face to look at him. She kept her eyes on a spot somewhere on her father's shirt. *What would it be like to be inanimate? To be a button, perhaps?*

'Learn a trade then. Tailoring. Hairdressing. Anything instead of sitting around all day like a retired grandmother,' her mother said, materializing beside her husband, her voice clipped and impatient. Grace had no interest in either tailoring or hairdressing. She could not stand the thought of spending another year in secondary school. She wanted to be left alone; she wanted for her life to roll backwards to the year before it all began to unravel.

'Anyway, you can't just sit home getting fatter and fatter,' her father snapped. 'We are trying to help you, but you, Grace, you need to help yourself too.' He finally moved away from the TV and warned Grace not to turn it back on. Grace said nothing. She did what she had been doing since the night she was forced to give up Baby. She sat and she sulked and fed her hate. Grace discovered that when she scraped back her anger (at herself, at Ben and at their parents), what she was left with was hate. And that hatred grew each day she saw her parents living as if life was normal, and imagined Ben and his parents doing the same. She watched her parents sit in front of the news and eat the dinner that she made while they were at work, discussing Abacha this and Abacha that, and how much things were deteriorating under this president and would the country ever see a civil rule, and she hated them with everything in her body. Their discussions angered Grace who wanted them to once, just once, talk about Baby. When she could no longer stand to hear her parents whine about her future over and over again, she went in for midwifery. It was a relatively short course, she would be easily employable, and she could leave and never have to see her parents again. If she didn't have to rely on them for money, if she had her own, she could have a different life. She was already determined that once she got a job, she would find her own place and never set foot in her parents' house again. She had managed all that. When she spoke of her parents, she spoke of them in the past tense. To everyone she met from the day she started earning her own money, her parents were dead. But now her mother had dragged herself from the dead, shed her ghostliness and appeared alive and solid in Grace's parlour.

Five

New Lay Out, Enugu

2020

Grace's life began to fall apart the day her mother returned from the dead, resurrecting in Grace's living room, an apparition smelling of flowers and soup as if the pact she and Grace had made was nothing. On the radio and TV, people were still being warned that there was a pandemic, but for Grace and many others, little had changed. At the clinic, she had had a normal day. No surprise deliveries, no emergencies requiring her ambulance to take a patient to the private hospital with which she had an arrangement, no overflowing toilets or burst pipes. And best of all, there were no surprise returns which would have been problematic. After all, she did not run a clothes boutique – where returns would not even be accepted – but a sought-after maternity service. Luckily, it had only ever happened once that a new parent returned a baby they'd gone home with.

The day her mother resurrected, nineteen years after Grace had last seen her, there were no unwanted babies to find new homes for. No crisis to deal with. It had just been a regular, normal day and Grace was looking forward to a long soak in the bath and an evening in with Okika. Maybe they would even make love without worrying about noise. The twins were at a friend's house for a sleepover weekend where the parents did not mind a bunch of teenagers getting together in the middle of a pandemic. There was nothing to suggest that when she walked into her living room at the end of the day, instead of a relaxed Okika playing something slow on the CD player, inviting her to dance with him like he often did, he'd be turned toward the door, a face like thunder, as if he had been sitting there all day just waiting for Grace to walk in so he could explode.

'What's wrong, babe?'

'You tell me,' Okika said, pointing his chin behind him towards a woman Grace had not yet had the time to notice. From the door, she couldn't see well. She definitely should stop resisting the glasses the optician had told her she needed. Yet even though Grace's sight wasn't sharp enough to see the woman who was sitting in front of the dining table, her heart knew immediately who it was.

'May the eyes with which I see you not kill me,' the woman said and began to walk towards Grace, a black cloth mask dangling from one ear. Just like her mother, Grace thought, to never go the full distance. She'd wear a mask but only if she didn't have to actually put it on. It was the same when her mother had followed her to Ben's house but couldn't confront his parents. She had turned around and taken Grace with her. Did Ben's parents have two heads? Were they not human beings like her mother? Grace's surprise was congealing into anger. Anger at the woman who had let her teenage daughter carry the burden of Baby. Grace wanted to yank the offending mask off her mother's face.

Grace had been saying that her parents were dead for so long that she had come to believe it. For that reason, the first thought that filtered through the confusion of seeing her mother in her house – before the anger – was that she was a ghost. Grace stood rooted on the spot, near the front door, unable to come any further into the room. She would wonder later how her mother had found her, but then would realize that someone like her, a society woman, whose face was in the papers and on TV, was not exactly hiding. Enugu wasn't Lagos. Even with all of its expansions, it was still a small city. Anyone who knew her, and wanted to find out where she lived would be able to. But right at this moment, the why and how did not consume her as much as what she would tell Okika. If the mother she'd told him was dead was in fact alive, what else could she be hiding from him? If she told him everything else – about Baby – what would that mean for them? For her? Suddenly, Grace felt a tightening in her chest, a weakening of her knees, and made her way unsteadily into the room and sank her body gently into a chair.

Six

New Haven, Enugu

1993

Ben started sneaking Grace into his house when his parents were away so they could spend more time together. Grace did not fight him. In fact, she wanted it. She might not have been able to go to night parties with him, but she had to show him that she could be like Patience, or as grown-up as he needed her to be. So she told her parents she had study meetings with classmates, the lie rolling smoothly off her tongue, easy like the love she felt for Ben. She hoisted her schoolbag on her shoulders and made her way to the back of the house where Ben waited to walk with her to his. The young love birds did not mind the sun, the heat, the stench of the gutters on their thirteen-minute walk from Chime Avenue to Byron Onyeama Close, Grace walking behind Ben as if they were not together, and up to Ituku Street where they finally held hands once they passed the psychiatric hospital, and ran towards Ben's secluded family home and privacy. If she could, she would skip all the way to Ben's where the world was just the two of them. All through the short trip, when she trailed him like a stranger so no wandering eyes would see her and report back to her parents, she felt the pull of him like a magnet. The first few times at his house they kissed, biting each other lightly on the lips. How could anyone's lips be so soft, Grace wondered. She could live in her boyfriend's kiss forever. Ben wanted more. The kissing was good but what if he could see her breasts too? 'Please, Gracie, let me see your breasts. Just a quick peek. I can show you mine if you want to see too.' At first she giggled and said no. 'Plus you have nothing to show. You don't even have breasts, sef,' she said. Then he begged, and told her he loved her, and she loved him, and they were boyfriend and girlfriend, right? 'What's the big deal, eh, Gracie?' And Grace had to admit that it was no big deal. It was just her breasts he wanted to see; it wasn't like he was asking her to strip naked for him, which she would never do, tufia! Not in a million years. She would never *nakedize* herself in front of a boy even if that boy was her boyfriend. And so she raised her top so he could see her breasts, trapped in her brassiere. When he reached out to touch them, Grace shuddered. Her knees wobbled and she thought she might faint. From then on, every time she came to visit, Ben would touch her breasts, cupping them while they kissed, sometimes slipping a hand through her bra to touch her skin and pinch her nipples. Grace had not known all these ways in which her body could delight her. At night, while she lay in bed, safely shielded from her parents' watchful eyes, she replayed everything in her mind, ran her hands over her bra, pretending that her hands were Ben's, and imagined Ben calling her name over and over. Gracie. Gracie. Like something sweet and full and delightful. One day Ben asked if she wanted to see him naked. She said no, God forbid, and giggled nervously. Why would she want to see him naked? Only bad girls saw boys naked and she wasn't a *bad* girl.

'I'd show you if you asked.'

'No, thank you,' she said.

'You want to remove your clothes and show me? I want to see your boobs well.'

Grace giggled and said God forbid. Letting him touch her breasts under her clothes was one thing, but removing her clothes for him? Embarrassment would kill her. 'Okay. Okay,' Ben said. 'Do you want to eat something?' And Ben brought in some chin-chin and some groundnuts, which they always had in abundance in his house where they had everything – including a washing machine and a dryer! Grace often thought of how lucky Ben was to live in this house where his parents were not constantly breathing down his neck, where the cupboards never ran dry of snacks and soft drinks, and where the kitchen was like something out of a foreign magazine complete with a microwave. Grace's parents were not poor, but they did not have the wealth that could entertain such frivolous luxuries. When she and Ben grew up, she was determined that they would have even more.

Two weeks later, she and Ben were in the backyard of his house while Ben watered plants. He filled a bucket of water and strolled from plant to plant splashing a bit of it at a time. Grace said something she no longer remembered, teasing Ben. They began to mock fight and Ben ended up upending the bucket of water on her, drenching her, plastering her dress to her body.

'Ben! See what you've done now!' She panicked. If

she went home in wet clothes, she would have some explaining to do. She could not think of a single good excuse for her parents. 'What do I do?' She was almost crying. If her parents ever found out where she had been, they'd kill her. She'd be banned from ever stepping out of the house until she got married. She'd be flogged with a cane treated with pepper. 'What do I do, kwanu? Stand in the sun?' She was getting angry now.

'Remove them, let me put them in the dryer. They'll dry very quickly. Now-now even.'

'No!' She pushed him away as he tried to get her out of her skirt. 'I'm not removing my clothes.'

Ben raised his hands as if in surrender. 'I'm sorry. I'm sorry, Gracie, but what are you going to do then?'

'Just negodu? Just see, eh?' She pointed at her dripping self as if he could not see her.

'It was an accident. I'm sorry. Please, let me dry the clothes. Let's go inside. Please, Gracie, don't be angry with me. It was an accident.' He sounded hurt. Grace thought of walking home, her clothes all damp. She could already imagine her parents' relentless questioning under which she would buckle and tell the truth. And so she let Ben drag her to his room. And she let him help her shed her clothes. And Grace forgot in that moment to be embarrassed that she was standing in front of a boy only in her underwear. 'Those too,' Ben said, his voice somewhat choked.

'No!' No way was she going to remove them.

'Here.' He pulled the checkered top sheet off his bed. 'Tie this around you.' What was the point of drying her clothes and throwing them over wet lingerie? 'It doesn't make sense,' Ben said. Grace agreed that he was right.

She took the sheet, tied it around her body and slipped out of her underwear. Ben took her clothes into the bathroom where the dryer was. When he returned, he was shirtless. 'My shirt got wet from carrying your clothes,' he said. His voice sounded odd. 'Come, sit.' He sat on his bed and patted the space beside him. Grace sat, uncomfortably aware that she was naked underneath the sheet. Ben removed his glasses, threw them behind him on the bed and inched closer to her. 'Are you still angry with me?' She didn't answer. She was more uncomfortable than angry. Ben touched her neck. 'Gracie?' Silence. He traced her collarbone with one finger. 'Gracie?' He touched her face, began to kiss her. Then his hands strayed down to her breasts. She pushed him back.

'Why not? I've seen your boobs before. I'm just touching. Not even touching the real thing.'

'Don't.'

'Are you still angry with me? I'm sorry. It was an accident.'

He sounded hurt so she told him she was not angry and she let him touch her breasts over the sheets.

'You like it?'

'Yes.' She did.

'Push the sheets down so I can see them well.'

Grace pushed the sheet down to bare her breasts and could not believe the fire between her legs when Ben trapped a nipple between his teeth and tugged at it lightly before covering it with his mouth and beginning to suck like a baby. She was scared of the fire, but it delighted her too and she was stuck between wanting to ask him to stop and wanting him never to stop. And by the time the sheet was off and Ben himself was naked and she was coming to her senses and she told him to *stop, stop, stop*, her voice was too much of a squeak for him to hear. Afterwards, when he lay on top of her, great sobs racked her body. 'We are boyfriend and girlfriend, Gracie, don't cry, okay?' Ben said, rolling off her. When she would not, could not, stop crying, Ben tilted her face towards his. He wiped off her tears and teased her. 'But you enjoyed it, did you not? I could feel it.' Grace was not sure. She had some pain between her legs. She had wanted him to stop. 'I could feel you enjoying it,' Ben said again. He was smiling. 'Don't pretend ooo, Gracie.' He kissed her on the nose. Grace thought then that maybe she did. And if she hadn't enjoyed it, that she ought to have. Ben was her boyfriend after all. 'Yes. Yes, I enjoyed it.' And she nodded and said it again, feeling surer the more she said it. In the days that followed, every chance Ben got to bring her over to his, they did what boyfriends and girlfriends did. Having done it once, there was no need to stop, was there, Ben asked Grace. She did not agree but Ben was so convincing, and he loved her so much. He showered her with gifts. With affection. With love. He sneaked notes through her classroom window telling her how much he loved her. *My moon. The only girl for me.* She scribbled back and sneaked her responses into his school bag when they walked home from school. *My stars. The only boy for me.* They would marry once they were old enough. After university and once settled in good jobs. She wanted to be a dentist. He was going to be a lawyer. And they would have five children. No, two. No, four. When her seditious heart tried to tell her that their relationship had changed in ways she was not always comfortable with, she quieted it with the reminder that

Ben was her boyfriend, they would marry in the future, so there was nothing wrong with what they were doing. It was like eating your lunch at breakfast. The timing might be wrong, but it was still your food and you were still going to eat it at some point. And when she wasn't giving in to the discomfort, she found that she too quite enjoyed being with Ben in that way, enjoyed the way he told her that there was no other girl at school or elsewhere who came close to her in beauty. 'We will have beautiful children,' he said. She pushed away all her misgivings, the voice of her mother telling her that good girls did not let boys see them naked, the dread that was always trailing her enjoyment, and said that yes, they would have beautiful children, their faces shiny with good living.

Seven

New Haven, Enugu

1993

It was Grace's mother who first noticed that Grace was moving slower, getting puffy in the face and becoming unable to stand the smell of okra soup. She asked Grace if she had a fever. 'Your face is shining too much. Must be malaria,' her mother said and gave her two tablets of chloroquine to fold into her eba and swallow to stave off the fever. But when, early on a Sunday morning, Grace ran out of the kitchen, gagging because the smell of the stockfish turned her stomach, her mother squinted at her as if she could no longer see her properly and asked her when her last period was. Grace could not remember. Her mother dragged her by the ear and asked her to tell her who had made her pregnant. Grace, stunned – she had never, ever thought she could get pregnant – pressed her lips together. Around her, the house swayed and a storm gathered in her mother's face and the heavens emptied themselves on Grace's head, the wooden spoon with which her mother had been stirring soup was thunder striking her cheeks. 'Who did this, Grace? Eh? Who did you allow to come between your legs?' Grace said nothing.

Her mother did not ask her a second time. 'Papa Grace,' her mother shouted, going in search of her husband, the spoon still in one hand like a weapon. With the other hand, she dragged Grace by her wrist. Grace's father was in the sitting room reading a newspaper. 'Papa Grace, our enemies have won ooo! Your daughter is pregnant.' He dropped the newspaper as if it had suddenly become hot. He looked from his wife to Grace. 'How? How can you know boys in that way? At your age?' Grace watched in alarm as his face folded and he began to cry. She had never seen her father cry, had thought it an impossibility. Fathers – men – did not cry. Grace was embarrassed. As if she was witnessing something she should never have to. And then she felt guilty for being responsible. Her father often teased her by calling her his 'favourite daughter', and even though she was an only child, his voice carried the conviction of truth. She was convinced that, had she had siblings, she would have still been her father's favourite. He'd wanted her to be a doctor, but she was put off medicine by the idea of dissecting cadavers. Her ambition to be a dentist was partly a compromise to make her father happy. If he wanted a doctor child, she would give him one. Whenever she topped the class, he insisted on celebrating. On Saturdays, they played card games together. She didn't know any other father who spent time with their children like he did with her. She couldn't bear to look at him.

'Who did this?' her mother asked again. Shame sewed Grace's lips shut. If only she could leave, she would go to Ben, and he would know how to make things right. If only her mother, whose nails were digging into her wrist, would let her go. Ben had told her their lovemaking would not have any consequences. She had taken a bath each time, as soon as she came home, like he'd told her to, scrubbing thoroughly between her legs with hot water and salt. Ben said one of his older brothers had told him it worked to keep away pregnancy. His brother would know; he was experienced. Grace had . . .

Thwack! Like an unexpected raindrop, the back of the wooden spoon landed near her temple. Grace let out a shriek and brought her free hand to her head to soothe it. The spoon landed on the back of her hand next. 'Which useless person did this?' *Thwack!* 'Who.' *Thwack.* 'Did.' *Thwack.* 'This?' *Thwackthwackthwack.* Eventually, her mother had beaten Ben's name out of her. And his address. Grace had not even been able to tell Ben (how could she?) before her mother hauled her to his house to see his parents to, as she put it, 'set things right. Even useless schoolboys must do the right thing!'

When Grace and her mother returned from Ben's that Sunday morning, Grace's father was still on the same couch in the living room, his newspaper on the table where he had flung it earlier, as if he hadn't moved at all since they left. 'And?' her father asked. There was a deep silence into which the ceiling fan above them whirred. Grace shifted in her chair so that she did not have to look at her mother's face. Her mother sighed. A long hmmm. 'Papa Grace, the insult your daughter made me eat, eh? My mouth cannot even say it.' Grace's mother slapped her thighs as if the insult were a mosquito she was slapping to death. She shook her head, her braids swaying from side to side. 'Ah! Papa Grace. The insult is still sitting in my stomach.' Grace knew her mother was remembering sitting in the opulent parlour of Ben's parents with wall-to-wall carpeting so soft and deep it was like walking onto a field of cotton wool. 'Your house is very fine,' she'd told Ben's parents. Grace sat down next to her mother, wanting the floor to open up and swallow her. The maid that had let them in recognized Grace. She had seen her a few times at the house. She gave Grace a quick smile, knelt in greeting to Grace's mother and went down a long corridor to call her bosses, her slippers slapping noisily against her heels, the noise getting further and further away from the visitors until a door opened somewhere in the womb of the passage. Grace and her mother stood quietly, not saying a word to each other. Soon, Grace could hear Ben's father, whom she had never met, grumble about early-morning callers and his mother, whom Grace had also never met, say something in response. They did not sound happy, but when they came into the parlour, suddenly appearing as if they had been spat out by the hallway, they smiled in greeting. 'Sit down. Sit down,' Ben's mother said, sinking into a chair that seemed more like a throne with arms carved like lion heads. His father remained standing. He had a wrapper tied around his waist, a pot belly hanging over it. Grace and her mother sat. 'Your house is very fine,' her mother repeated.

'Thank you. My husband and I like it very much.' Ben's mother's voice was very polite, even though Grace could hear underneath that politeness a temptation to ask her mother to get to the point, to tell her why two strangers were in her house so early on a Sunday morning.

'Very fine.'

'Would you like something to drink? It's so early, it's difficult to know what to offer.' Ben's mother crossed her legs. She didn't sound like she wanted to offer them anything. Grace saw how much Ben looked like his mother. The slim nose with a droopy nostril she sometimes teased him about before they kissed. She wondered where he was, if he was still sleeping. She had never seen the house this full; she could not even remember sitting in the parlour, they were often busy doing other things. Despite everything, despite the severity of their errand that morning, a smile tucked itself into her cheek. If Ben came out – once Ben came out – everything would be alright. He would know what to do. Her mother had said that the way these things were done, he would have to marry her. Grace did not want to get married now; God forbid. And she did not think Ben wanted to, either. Nobody their age got married. How funny it would be to turn up to school as husband and wife. The image made Grace forget where she was and why, and she let out a chuckle. All three pairs of eyes turned towards her. Her mother's warned her to *behave or else*.

'The thing is that . . .' Grace's mother started, her voice tremulous. She cleared her throat. She began again. 'Our people say that a dead body does not hide from the person who will bury it.' Ben's mother looked puzzled, as if she needed the proverb explained to her. Ben's father nodded. A slow nod as if he were Pete Edochie in a Nollywood film and had been instructed by the director to nod sagely. Silence. Everyone waited for Grace's mother to continue. 'We are here – me and my daughter – because your son, Ben, got her pregnant.' Ben's father, who had been standing looking at them, turned his head towards a cavernous hallway behind him as if the words were an unexpected slap on his face. He shouted for the house girl, Caro, to bring his breakfast into the bedroom for him. 'Bring it now, now. Let me eat and go to church.' He knotted the ends of his wrapper and, without saying a word to anyone, he walked back the way through which he had come, swallowed in the belly of the corridor. It seemed to Grace that a girl's pregnancy was the business of mothers. Ben's mother clapped her hands as if she was applauding Grace and then with a sneer asked her, 'How old are you?'

'Fifteen, ma.'

'Speak up. I can't hear you. If you're old enough to get pregnant, you're old enough to speak so I can hear.'

'Fift . . . fifteen, ma.'

'Fifteen. I hail you ooo.' She raised a fist in mock salute to Grace, standing up as she did so.

'Fifteen and pregnant!' She sat down again and turned to Grace's mother. 'You bring your nonsense daughter here to do what? Ben is sixteen. You think he will marry her? And if she's spreading her legs for him, how many other boys is she spreading them for? Butter legs. Sharer.'

'Madam . . .' Grace's mother tried to interject but Ben's mother raised a hand, palm out to stop her.

'It's not my fault you raised such a little prostitute. Leave my house. Nonsense!' She turned to Grace. A finger wagging at the young girl, she delivered a stern warning, promising to chop off her legs if she stepped foot on their property again, spitting on Grace as she stood, immobile and dazed, until her mother grabbed her by the hand and pulled her away. Grace and her mother could still hear her shouting to their backs, threatening fire and brimstone as they walked out the door and began the long walk home.

Now, Grace could not bear to look at her father. She could not handle his silent accusation, his crying. She wished he would shout at her and beat her like her mother did, punish her in some way to reduce the guilt she was carrying. Since Ben's parents would not do the right thing, her mother said, they would have to do something. And quickly too. It was a blessing, she said, that Grace had always been a shiny, big girl; people were not likely to notice before they had a chance to fix things. 'Papa Grace,' she said tenderly. 'Biko, stop crying. And you.' She turned to Grace. 'Get out of my sight.'

Eight

New Haven, Enugu

1993

At school the next day, Ben walked right by Grace as if she was invisible.

That evening, when Grace returned home, her mother gave her two pills she had pilfered from the hospital where she worked as a nurse. 'Here. These will sort you out. O ga-adicha mma. Everything will be alright.' Tiny and yellow, the colour of urine. Her mother's hand trembled as she held the drugs out to Grace, as if the tablets were a living, squirming animal. Grace pinched the tablets between her fingers, marvelling at how tiny they were – smaller even than chloroquine, which she took each time she got malaria – and swallowed them. Then she waited for the magic they would release inside her, the miracle that would right her world and stop it from completely tipping over. Even though she did not like taking pills, she trusted her mother. And more than anything, Grace wanted to go back to not being pregnant, to not being afraid that other children in the neighbourhood or school would notice and mock her, to her parents not looking at her as if she was no longer Grace but a foreigner who had wandered into their home and for whom they provided but could not talk to.

That night, Grace woke up with cramps that had her shouting for her mother. She thought she was going to die. The pain was like nothing she had ever experienced. Pincers pinching her intestines. Giant fingers wringing them like wet washing. Her mother got her a hot-water bottle to lie on top of and sat with her, kneading her back. This was the mother she had known before she became pregnant. Her mother put Grace's head in her lap and stroked her cheeks. Grace felt her whole body thrumming with happiness. She did not mind that she was sick. She did not mind that the pills squeezed her insides so hard she was afraid she would pass out. That they made her so nauseous that she vomited several times and passed a little blood. Her mother cleaned up the sick and cleaned her up, humming a song she used to sing for Grace as a little child, as if Grace were that child again.

> *Nwa m ebezi na ebezi na*
> *Nne gi no nso, e bezi na.*
> *Do not cry child*
> *Your mother is here.*

The next day, Grace stayed home from school although the cramps had eased. Her head throbbed. Her mother gave her two Panadol tablets and told her to sleep in, that everything was fine now. Her mother sounded like her mother again. Her father kissed her on the forehead before he too left for work. 'It's all over now,' he said. 'Everything is fine.' And Grace believed it, because there was nothing her parents could not do.

But Grace's stomach kept growing, and this time she knew before her mother noticed that the pill had done nothing to reverse the fate that awaited her. It was too late to give her anything, her mother said when it became clear to her that her daughter was still pregnant. Grace could not imagine having a real, live child. What would she do with it? Some nights, she rubbed her hands across her belly and tried to imagine an entire human being nestling inside her. She could not. She thought of the pregnancy as something happening outside of herself. She did not know anyone her age who had become pregnant. She sniffed under her arm and was relieved that she smelled normal, like her deodorant. Aunty Maggie, her mother's cousin, pregnant at the time, had stayed with them for a while because hospitals in Enugu were better at handling whatever problem she had developed in pregnancy than the ones in Oguta where she lived, and she had had a distinctive odour. When Grace, who could not stand the smell, like the inside of someone's shoes, asked her mother why, she had been told that it was the smell of pregnancy. It had worried Grace that she would acquire the stench too, but so far, so good. She crossed herself.

When Grace thought of Ben, she felt something like heartburn. She banished herself to her room where she clattered around like a bug trapped in a bottle. She could not breathe there. It seemed like all of Enugu's heat, heavy and oppressive, gathered in that small room, and no matter how wide she threw her windows open, she could do very little to shift it.

Her mother played loud gospel music whenever she was home, banishing the devil that had entered their lives, she said. Her father read the papers. Grace stayed out of their way. She wore boubous and stayed hidden inside, coming out on the balcony only for short periods while her parents were at work. Once, a neighbour looked up and saw her and shouted 'Sorry' to her. Grace's parents had told people she had typhoid fever she couldn't seem to get over. Grace nodded and walked back inside, the baby a stump of wood inside of her, weighing her down. How could something that small be so heavy, she wondered. She ate whatever her mother served. She knew better than to mention her cravings: goat meat pepper soup, ugba and okporoko, fried snail. She imagined that she was someone else, someone older, living in her own house indulging in whatever she fancied. In those fantasies, her parents did not exist. And neither did this tenacious baby which her mother's pills had not managed to flush out.

Nine

Uwani, Enugu

2020

It was not often that Grace had couples coming to see her, and that was why this particular morning, seven months before her mother reappeared, had felt to her like a celebration. Often the men sent their wives alone, as if they wanted no part in it, as if they were ashamed to be seen collecting babies they had not sired. Grace did not understand it. This taboo around raising children that one did not birth. When she was young, she recalled, a wealthy couple from her town had thrown a party for their child. She remembered one of her mother's friends mocking the couple: 'Imagine throwing a party for a child they bought.' Grace's mother hadn't told the woman she was wrong. She had *ahhed* and *hmmed*, shaking her head at these unfortunate people who had had to resort to adoption. Later, after the visitor had left, Grace had asked her mother why it was such a bad thing. 'Blood,' her mother had said. Adopted children did not have one's blood, she said, and told Grace the story of the woman from their town who was rich but unmarried. She had adopted a boy and a girl, and once they were old enough, she had them marry each other. The woman left all her property to them. 'They could marry because no matter that they called the same woman "mother", they were not related. For a child to be your child, you have to share the same blood. You always want to know whose blood runs through the veins of your child. Better to remain childless than to adopt.' And better, apparently, to throw away a child than to have one outside of wedlock, Grace thought now. Grace did not blame people who chose to hide the fact that the baby they were raising wasn't theirs biologically. How can one person fight society? Better to pretend and lie and keep everyone away from your business. Grace was glad that not many people thought like her mother did anymore or else the babies she was placing would have no one to raise them.

Her mind turned again to the couple. When the wife had called, sounding girlish and excited, to make the appointment, Grace had wondered if the 'husband' was euphemism for a sugar daddy or a lover because she hardly ever had husbands accompany their wives, but the woman had said they were married, and they were coming together. A sugar daddy with a family elsewhere would not risk coming to the clinic during the day with his side chick. Those ones liked to operate in the dark, in hotels and motels far from the city. The wealthy ones planned holidays abroad so they could hold hands and eat out with their lovers. Grace had been even more astounded when the couple turned up. They were young: a lot younger than Grace's usual clientele. That first time they came to Grace's for a consultation, faces unlined and fresh, smelling of expensive eau-de-something, they looked out of place sitting opposite Grace, not asking to be taken in because the woman was pregnant and could not keep the baby, not needing her help in that way. 'We'd like a baby, six to nine months from now,' the woman who'd introduced herself as Christine said. 'We've been told that you're the one to see,' her husband said. Most of Grace's clients were referrals. She was a trained midwife; she had doctors and nurses working for her and ran a full maternity hospital, but hardly any pregnant woman came to her for services they could get elsewhere. They came for her unadvertised services. Mostly those who came, willing to pay the huge premium Grace demanded for infants, were much older than these two in T-shirts and jeans. They were most likely in their late twenties. The woman was more the age of those Grace called the 'Givers'. Often pregnant and alone and poor, the Givers came to Grace to save them from a fate worse than being pregnant and alone. She was curious about Christine and her husband, Charles. These two couldn't have been married long. Christine did not have the look of the put-upon wife, surrounded by adversarial in-laws harassing her for a child, so what was their hurry? She wanted to tell them to enjoy their youth, enjoy each other's company, travel, see the world before adding a baby to that equation. They seemed happy together, they laughed a lot, everything seemed to set them off, even when they were being serious. Charles spoke with an accent she could not place, something foreign but not any of the easily placeable ones like British or American. There was something about them, a fondness that did not strike Grace as sexual. They touched each other when they spoke, but the touches lacked an energy she associated with being young and in love. They'd been married for a year, Christine offered. 'And we need to show my parents a child or we lose everything,' Charles said. A year? There was none of the spark of a new marriage, yet this was a couple who genuinely seemed to revel in each other's company. And why the rush? A year was nothing. Grace did not ask what they might lose. An inheritance? Christine said his parents still lived abroad, in France. Hers were in Abuja. They'd told both sets she was pregnant, and she planned to wear an adjustable fake pregnancy silicone belly. The sooner they could get the baby business out of the way, the better for everyone all round, she said. They shared a smile that seemed to hold a secret. Of all her clients so far, these were the ones she was most curious about. Grace considered the propriety of probing, and discarded the thought. Six months later, they came to collect their son, a boy, born a week late. The couple had insisted on meeting with their 'surrogate' as soon as someone suitable turned up. A month after their first 'consultation', Grace called them in to meet a shy teenager, Anwuli, who had been brought in by her mother, begging for help.

Anwuli had missed her period, her mother said. She was sure her daughter was pregnant and if Grace could not help them, their life was finished. Anwuli's mother smelled of firewood and mothballs. She wiped her eyes with the back of her hand like a child as she spoke, her voice breaking. 'We have never harmed anyone, not one. Our only crime is being poor.' She shook her head and blew her nose into the mask covering the lower part of her face. She looked embarrassed, whispered a 'sorry', took off the mask and stuffed it into her bag. Grace handed her another mask from the pile she kept behind her for people who came to her without one. She wasn't taking any chances with the pandemic. 'Of all the girls in Agbor, the devil chooses my daughter to try.' Grace had been shocked to hear that they'd come from so far away. How had they heard of her, she asked. The woman grunted. 'The uncle who did *this*,' she said. 'We don't know how he knows of this place, but he came to us and said he had a solution for our problem.' She hissed. '*Our* problem, as if he's not to blame. He raped my daughter. Ah!' Anwuli stared at a spot above Grace's head. She still had not said a word. Grace's heart went out to her. 'Why don't you report him?' Grace asked before she could stop herself. Neither the girl nor her mother answered. It was a foolish question. To whom would they report a man who kept them fed? The girl's father was a driver who worked for this 'uncle', who was not a relative. He was a wealthy man; they lived in a flat he gave his employees and so their hands were tied. He would give them money for an abortion, or they could bring Anwuli to Enugu and let her have the child away from view, and give the baby away. Either way, he did not want his name mixed up in whatever they chose to do. He had a wife, he had children. If he heard that they spread this 'nonsense' of him getting their daughter pregnant, Agbor would not be big enough to contain their two families. Abortion scared Anwuli and scared her mother, who had nightmares of her daughter's death on an operating table. Grace knew men like this 'uncle'. How many other girls was he getting away with raping? She'd take the girl, she said.

'You have nothing to worry about. We will look after her, make sure she gets the best care.' And because she felt sorry for the woman, Grace broke her own rules. She counted out N30,000 and slid it across the table to Anwuli's mother. 'After the baby is born, your daughter will get the balance.' The woman got up and began to do a little jiggle. Their only desire, she said, was to get their daughter out of the trouble he'd put them in. And to hear that they'd even get some money in the process made it all the more bearable. 'God bless you, ma. God bless you.'

From the beginning, Christine wanted to spend time with Anwuli, something many of the other 'parents' didn't do. She wanted to know everything about the girl, her symptoms, her pains. Christine had studied Theatre Arts, Charles said. 'When she takes on a role, she inhabits it.' 'Same as you, darling husband,' Christine said, laughing. Grace felt as if she was being left out of an inside joke. The seventeen-year-old carrying their child did not mind. They had got on well and for them, Grace had made an exception. They'd come to the clinic often, bearing gifts of food and comics for the girl. Assaulted, and sworn to silence by her parents to avoid the shame, Anwuli appreciated their visits. Her own family members would not come. 'And why not?' Grace overheard Christine ask her once. 'They are far away,' the girl said, 'and this is not normal. After the baby is out, I'll go home. My mother says it would be as if it never happened.' Grace did not want to think of what might have happened to this girl had her mother not brought her to the clinic that day, tired and worn out after a bus ride from Agbor. Christine and Charles had wanted to do more than just give her money. They wanted her in school. 'We'll pay the school fees,' Charles said. 'For as long as she wants to stay in school. And we'll give her an allowance.'

'And she can live with us, as the nanny if she wants,' Christine said. Grace did not think that was a good idea, but it wasn't her place to say. This business worked because there were no ties between birth mother and new parents – no meeting, no nothing. She handled the business side of things. But Christine and Charles were not her normal clientele. They were different in a way she couldn't exactly pinpoint. Maybe it was their age – they were full of idealism; they wanted to save the world. They spoke of eco this and eco that, climate chaos and toxicity. They felt guilty, they said, taking this baby, and if they didn't need to, they wouldn't, and they couldn't without doing right by its mother. Did the girl have no family who wanted to see the child at least? They wanted a clean break from the baby, Anwuli's mother said. She and Anwuli were happy to have the couple send Anwuli to school. 'But she cannot live with the baby,' her mother said. She took the money Grace gave her, bundles of it, and stuffed it into a polythene bag she'd brought, tied it up and put it at the bottom of a travel bag. She took the extra Christine gave her. She knelt down in front of Grace and Christine and Charles and thanked them over and over again. 'May your purses never run dry.' She left the card with their phone number and address which Charles had insisted on giving her: 'In case you ever want to see the baby. We won't mind, I promise. I am . . . we are so sorry.' His voice cracked. Grace looked on like a proud mother. She had delivered a child to a family that wanted one and had saved a girl that most likely would have had her life ruined but was now going to be able to finish her education. Her family would not need to be beholden to the predator 'uncle' if things worked out. Pride was a sin, Grace thought, but everyone needed a vice. And it was pride that was deserved, was it not?

★ ★ ★

She felt the fullness that settled in her stomach like a good meal each time a baby was collected, but there were always other women, many more young girls waiting to deliver babies. So many, in fact, that Grace had had to become more stringent with those she accepted. Not long after, she had to turn a pregnant girl away. The girl came in alone, hair tangled and her eyes red and watery. Grace did not want the liability of an addict. And who was to say that the girl's addiction hadn't harmed the baby? What would she do with a baby no one wanted? She was running a business, not a home. And how had the girl even found her? 'I was just looking. Looking for a hospital. The government hospital won't take me. A nurse. She asked me to come here.' The girl's teeth were chipped and brown. Her nails were dirty. Her speech was garbled. 'I am sorry,' Grace said. When the girl started crying and refused to move, Grace had summoned one of the two policemen permanently stationed outside the clinic's gates. He had dragged the girl, screaming and wailing, out of the building. It was painful to watch, Grace admitted to her friend Ifeatu later. 'But what was I to do?' She did not tell Okika. She hardly ever told him anything about her work. He was always quick to judge in that quiet voice of his. He even chastised her for using the police as her personal security, as if he wasn't Nigerian, as if he didn't know that anyone who wanted to and could afford it could have their own on-site cops. Grace did not think often of that girl, but now, she wondered if it was bad karma. Turning away a girl that needed help because she didn't want to be inconvenienced. What if that girl had given birth and thrown the baby away? Maybe this was Grace's punishment, her mother turning up at her door.

Ten

New Lay Out, Enugu

2020

The day before Grace's mother turned up at her door, she had had the dream of the baby again.

The one she herself bundled up and left by the roadside like a heap of rubbish because her parents had left her no choice. And neither had Ben's. For days, Ben's mother's warning had rung in her ears. 'Useless girl, spreading your legs open for a boy at your age. If I see your legs here again, I'll chop them off.' At that age, she had believed the woman. The wealthy could do anything; they lived by other rules. Ben hadn't spoken up for her. If he had said a single word in support of her, his parents might have acted differently. The world did not treat boys as it did girls. Even this long after, she would not forgive him. Ninety-nine and on her deathbed, softened by age and a good life, she would still think that were he standing in front of her, wrinkled and old like her, she would spit on him. He could have kept the baby, and his life would never have changed. If he had told his parents he wanted the child, that he was going to marry Grace in the future like they said they would, his parents would have been unable to shame Grace and her mother the way they had. Grace hated him. She imagined, after abandoning the baby, running into Ben and stabbing him with a knife – that was how much she hated him. But she never did and, soon after, her parents had moved the family to another part of town, enrolled her in a new school where there was no chance of her seeing Ben ever again. They could all pretend, in their new neighbourhood, that the pregnancy had never happened. She was a regular sixteen-year-old in SS1, a bit older than her classmates, a certain hardness to her eyes that discouraged friendship. She tried to throw herself into her studies but Baby's face, the weight of her newborn body in Grace's hands, the warmth of her skin, haunted Grace so much that it was difficult for her to study. At home, she and her parents said little to each other. Their shared secret was a burden on their tongues and they did not speak for fear of it skittering out. At night, when she slept, Baby came to Grace in her dreams and Grace would stumble awake convinced that she had not been asleep, so vivid was it, always. Those mornings, it took her a while to get her heartbeat back to normal. Once, years later, she jumped out of bed, waking her husband, and running to the front door to retrieve the grizzling baby she was sure would be there. Of course, there was no baby. There never was. And had there been one, it wouldn't be the one she dreamed of constantly. If she lived, Baby would be a young woman now, an adult version of the infant in Grace's dreams. Grace would not even know how to look for her or where to start. No one had seen Grace that night, she was sure of it. And her mother had told her neither she nor Grace's father wanted to know what she was going to do or where she would do it; she only had to ensure that she did not get caught. 'You got yourself in this mess, you get yourself out of it,' her mother had said, shooing her out the door so quickly it seemed like her mother was afraid of changing her mind. Although they never spoke of it, there had been times, in the early days, when it appeared as if her parents – her father especially, who had resolutely kept away from any of the decisions – had been on the verge of asking, but they always hesitated, drew a curtain over it and talked about other things, mostly things she had to do.

'Chop me some onions.'
'Go to the market and grind beans.'
'Get me my slippers from the room.'
'Say your prayers.'
'Make a big pot of jollof.'
'Go study for your exams.'
'Lift your feet and walk smart, stop dragging them like someone's old wife.'

Grace obeyed her parents because she had no choice, but she hated them too, as much as she hated Ben. Once it was clear that the baby was going to be born, her parents could have protected it. Grace's mother often spoke of a cousin of hers who had a baby in her early fifties – 'Except we all knew it wasn't her baby. Her unmarried daughter had gone and got pregnant and the mother had pretended that the baby was hers. Hm. She thought she could deceive us. She'd told another cousin of ours when she started menopause, so how could she have got pregnant?' That was love, Grace thought. Why hadn't her own mother done the same for her? They had managed to keep her pregnancy hidden; her mother could have saved her daughter the shame of being an unwed mother by claiming the baby as hers. When a dissenting voice whispered to Grace that her mother would have had to pretend to have been pregnant too, Grace squashed it.

On this day, before her mother drifted back into her life, Grace had once again woken and rushed from the room to the door to rescue the baby she was sure, in her sleep-induced state, was there. She opened the door to a gust of cool air. She realized where she was and walked back into the bedroom, the scarf on her head slipping to cover one eye. She pushed it aside and slid back into the bed, the baby's cries singeing her ears and stinging her eyes.

'Where's the fire, babe?' Okika asked. She mumbled something vague about a parcel she was expecting from Jumia. Okika grunted, turned onto his side and continued to sleep. He hadn't thought to wonder why she would be expecting a parcel so early in the day.

The dreams Grace had were always the same, so that they seemed like one single, long dream playing on a loop every time she fell asleep. A baby swaddled in a piece of cloth, dumped at her front door, her cries loud enough to wake the neighbourhood. She knew in the dream that if she did not take the baby inside it would die, but every time she reached out for it, she would wake up. There was a particular cruelty to these dreams that forced her to mourn Baby over and over with the rawness of new loss, a stain she could not expunge no matter how many new babies she helped in her clinic, inhaling their new-baby smell as she had done with Kaikele and Mmuodum, sometimes singing them a lullaby: *Nwa nnunu, nwa nnununta turuzanza turunza.* Grace had borne her enduring grief stoically, quietly, year after year for twenty-six years. Now, she was going to lose everything because of her mother. Grace felt as if she, Grace, was all the trees in a bushfire that was out of control, about to be completely incinerated.

Eleven

New Lay Out, Enugu

2020

Okika sat as still as a tree as Grace's mother spoke. Grace wished he would say something, throw something, do anything but sit there looking at her as if she were a stranger. It was a blessing that the girls were away and that Cee, the woman who doubled as cook and housekeeper, was off for the weekend. Grace would have hated for anyone to witness this unravelling of her life. How had this happened? Ben's family had sought out Grace's parents, wanting to know where to find their son's child. Grace's mother said they'd turned up early one Sunday morning, as if they were replaying Grace and her mother's visit years ago. 'This time, they did not look all high and mighty. They looked like wilted plants.' Grace's mother sounded somewhat smug. Grace had not thought of that visit, or of Ben's parents, in many years. It was Ben alone who occupied her mind. Several times during the day, she found herself wishing him ill. Lice to infest his scrotum. Maps of craw-craw on his skin.

'They think you cursed him. Ben's parents think you did something to their son.'

'That I did *what*?' She wanted her mother to leave. What was all this talk about Ben and his parents and now a curse? She'd fulfilled her obligations, transferred a monthly allowance to them like a dutiful child – they'd put her through school, after all, and there was no other sibling to care for them in their old age. Grace was not superstitious, but she had heard enough tales of adult children who paid the price for abandoning their parents. There was the one who lost every job he ever got. Another could never have the child she so badly wanted. 'I don't want you ever contacting me,' she'd said firmly. She'd meant it, but she knew that if they begged her, if they showed some remorse, if they told her that they were sorry for what happened to Baby, she would melt. Her father didn't even look up from the newspaper he was reading. Her mother hopped as if there were hot coals under her feet. She kept opening and closing her mouth like a fish struggling out of water, but she said nothing to Grace. Her father's unconcern emboldened her. 'You two are dead to me,' she spat out. 'But I'll do my duty by you.' And she had kept her promise. She'd told them when she was getting married – she had written to them – because even if she didn't want them back in her life, they deserved to know. She was not a wicked child, just a disappointed one. And then she had called them, because she was not a cruel daughter who only told her parents that their only child was getting married in a letter. The call was short, and as soon as she had delivered her news, she hung up. She did not want to hear whatever it was they had to say. The dead do not speak. The stipends she transferred to her parents' joint account had become more generous as her prosperity increased. She knew how difficult it was to survive in Nigeria on pensions that did not always get paid out. Once, she saw a pensioner on TV who complained that after years of civil service, he was being treated like deadwood. He had given the best of his life to service and now, when he was supposed to enjoy the retirement that was due him, he was forced to look for non-existent jobs to survive. 'So what do you do to keep body and soul together?' the journalist asked, sticking the microphone into the man's face. The man looked defeated. He said, 'I wash clothes. I go from house to house with my bucket and soap and see if anyone wants their clothes washed.' 'Clothes?' the journalist asked, incredulous. The man nodded. He looked sheepish, then said, 'Sometimes, women have given me their underwear to wash. I cannot refuse. I need the money.' Grace hated her parents, but she did not want them to suffer, and she also did not want to give them any reason to come looking for her. And yet here was her mother, dragging the past she had successfully buried into her sitting room with her husband there, listening in.

'They believe you cursed him for . . .' She quickly looked at Okika and paused.

'Biko, I did not curse anyone. Come and be going.' Her mother looked older than she remembered but her skin now shone with a glow that only those who lived in luxury could boast of. Grace had developed that sheen too. The women who came to her with purses heavy with money for a baby had that sort of sheen too. Something tugged at her heart. She remembered when she was ill with malaria or typhoid fever, and her mother had stayed home with her, hovering over her, answering to her every need even though she was already eleven and old enough to look after herself. But when it mattered, when she needed her, Grace thought, her mother had let her down. And now, when she had managed to kill her off, her mother had resurrected herself and come to spoil the life Grace had built for herself despite everything. What did she hope to achieve turning up like this? Okika said something that sounded like, 'Continue.' So Grace's mother did.

'He was married for several years but, even though there was nothing wrong with himself or his wife, nothing the several medical experts they visited could figure out, he could never get her pregnant. And then his death. It was a car accident but there was no other car involved, just his.'

'And so? What's that got to do with me? How's that my business? I didn't curse anyone.' Grace's voice was louder now. 'What's all this now? What do those people want from me?' Had she not wished him ill all those years? Maybe her thoughts *were* responsible. Or maybe his wife had fertility issues that the doctors had missed. Or maybe it was karma. 'Look, I honestly don't care,' Grace said, her voice rising higher than she had intended. Something wrapped itself around her throat. 'You have to go . . . Tell them this has nothing to do with me. I didn't curse anyone.'

'They want you to forgive him. They want to know if . . . They want to see you. To ask you to forgive them.'

'I didn't curse anyone. I don't even know how to. And he's dead, is he not? So what do they need my forgiveness for?'

'They said . . . their lives changed. They think it's your anger with them.'

'You need to go, please. Tell them this has nothing to do with me. His death, his childlessness, their change in fortune, all of that has nothing to do with me.' She found it difficult to swallow, and coughed. She could feel Okika's eyes on her but she couldn't think of him now. One thing at a time.

Twelve

New Lay Out, Enugu

2020

Grace was breathless. Words were coming out of her mouth, too fast and too loudly, but she had no idea what she was saying. She couldn't control it. Her vision was blurred, she felt disoriented. She was aware that she was still in her sitting room, that Okika and her mother were there, but she couldn't see them. Years ago, when one of her father's oldest friends died suddenly, her father had spent hours pacing the house, talking gibberish. Grace was maybe ten at the time, but she remembered how struck she had been that her father who rarely said much was suddenly possessed by a mania for words. Her mother had followed him around, telling him to 'Let it all out, dear. Let it all out.' Later, after her father had sat down and finally cried, her mother told Grace that he had been expressing his grief. 'Some losses require you to moan as soon they hit you; others make you mad first. Your father had to talk the insanity out or he would have ended up completely out of his senses.' Grace had spent days searching her father's face for signs of impending madness, because how could her mother be sure that he had 'talked it all out'?

She understood now how her father must have felt. The constriction in the throat that couldn't be swallowed down, it made its way up. It was unexpected, this grief that was ascending her throat and spewing out of her mouth and blinding her.

She hadn't loved Ben in years. The thin line between hate and love was crossed the moment he began to ignore her. And it grew after Baby. She hated him. She had spent years fantasizing about what she would do if she saw him again. *Ignore him. Claw his eyes out. Spit on him. Stab him.* So why did she feel this sense of loss that was spinning her round her own house? She pinned her arms against her stomach. Why did it feel empty inside, the way it had the night she got rid of Baby? Why did she care that he had married someone else? Loved her the way he had claimed to love Grace? Wanted a child with her? It couldn't be grief. Or even if it was grief, she told herself, it wasn't for him. It was for the opportunity she no longer had to get back at him somehow. It wasn't fair that he was dead before she had a chance to gloat to him about how well she was doing, before she had a chance to show off her family to him, before she had a chance to throw his apologies – because in her fantasies, he was always deeply, intensely remorseful – back at him. Her eyes began to clear, the eruption from her lips began to quieten and she sat on the floor, not caring that Okika was looking at her the same way she had looked at her father all those years ago. Her heart hurt, her jaw ached. She couldn't understand it, this pain in her body. The memories that came did so without any warning. She and Ben kissing behind the classrooms. She remembered how she had loved kissing him; how when she was with him they were the only two people in the world; how she wanted to show him off; how she felt whenever anyone at NHSS called her Ben's girlfriend. Then other memories flooded. Ben had betrayed her. Right from the very beginning. She recalled the incident with the water when he had slept with her the first time. She saw his face when he began to ignore her at school. The repulsion when their eyes met. Her mother had no right bringing her this news. She stood and faced her mother. 'What are you still doing here?'

Her mother stood.

'Don't go,' Okika said, his voice tight and overly polite. 'You're my mother-in-law. Stay. Let's get to know each other. I didn't even know . . .'

Grace looked at Okika. He ignored her. Her mother had the good sense to refuse. She had to go home to cook for her husband, she said; she could not trust the small boy who lived with them with the task.

'We moved. We are in Trans-Ekulu now.' She rattled off an address. 'Come. Come and see us sometime. Bring the . . .' She looked around the room, at the framed pictures on the wall. Of the wedding, of Grace and Okika and the girls, of the girls by themselves in matching jeans and white T-shirts. 'It'd be nice to . . . to meet our grandchildren. While we still can. Your father is ill. He'd love to see you.' She put her mask over her mouth, missing her nose. Typical, Grace thought. She watched from the window, swaying from nervous energy, as her mother walked down the driveway to the gate; watched as the gateman let her out; watched as she disappeared. And then she turned to face Okika.

Thirteen

New Lay Out, Enugu

2020

After her mother left, Grace slumped in her chair. It was as if her mother's visit had drilled holes in her so that she was like a colander, except what was being sieved through was her strength. She could feel a migraine creep in like an unwelcome guest. All she wanted to do was lie in a dark room and wait out the headache, but she couldn't do that. Okika was watching her with a wariness in his eyes as if she was some insane woman who had found her way into their house.

'So, your mother was dead but she's not anymore?' He was pacing the sitting room now, going round in circles like one of those wind-up toys Grace had bought for the girls when they were still toddlers. It was making her dizzy watching him, but what could she do? What did he want her to do? Deny that the mother she'd told him was dead was in fact alive? And so too was her father? And oh, the Ben that she was supposed to have cursed? She happened to have had a baby with him twenty-six years ago.

'Okika . . . Babe . . .' She stopped because her headache

was getting worse and because she did not know how to say what she had to say, or even where to start.

'I'm waiting.' Now he stopped in front of her. She sat up. Should she ask him to sit? Talk to him while he was standing over her like a parent standing over a child who'd been naughty, ready to deliver a lecture or a spanking? Her headache made thinking impossible. 'Babe. My head hurts. I just need—'

Okika cut in. 'Seriously?' The voice he'd been holding under control rose sharply. 'Seriously? We've been together, what? Eighteen years? Nineteen? We have children together, and I'm just finding out for the first time that you have a family? That the parents you said were dead are alive, and in Enugu, and you tell me your head is hurting? What the hell, Grace? What in the actual hell?'

'I'm sorry.' Grace's voice was a whisper. The headache was taking over, pounding in her head. She wished Okika wouldn't shout. She hadn't even known he had it in him to be this loud. She couldn't deal with this now, but what choice did she have?

'So, my parents are not dead. Obviously. But . . .'

'I'm listening.'

'Sit down, please.' The stripes on his trousers intensified the ache behind her eyes. They rippled, blurring into each other and making her vertiginous, but she couldn't very well tell him this now. This was not the Okika that she could reason with. 'Sit down, please, and I'll tell you everything.'

'No. I'm not sitting. Say what the hell you've got to say.' He was shouting even louder now, the veins on his neck standing out as if ready to pop. She had never heard him sound like this. Okika did not shout. He always complained that he did not understand why people thought shouting made them better heard. 'All I hear when people shout is just garble.' It was why he hated markets. On the few occasions they needed to go to Ogbete or main market and didn't want to send Cee, Okika always begged Grace to go instead. Yet here he was now, shaking the walls of the house with his voice, every word he dropped a hammer splintering her head.

Grace shut her eyes against the stripes and Okika's voice. She tried to will the words to come and the headache to go. She took a deep breath, held it. And she started. From the beginning. From meeting Ben to telling her parents they were dead to her. There was no need to leave anything out now. She told her story quickly so that she could be done and get something for the headache that was now consuming her. By the time she finished, it had gotten darker and Okika had neither moved nor said a word. Grace did not know what was going through his mind; she did not dare ask. She had always been able to tell Okika's mood, to say with certainty how he was going to react to something one way or the other, but now the man looking at her, staring at her, wasn't anyone she knew. It chilled her. She thought of the story of the Lagos businessman who discovered that his daughter was not biologically his and had murdered his wife. But before killing her, he'd tortured her. Pulling out her braids one at a time. And then he had stabbed her to death. The man had called his brother to say he'd done something terrible, but by the time the brother arrived, he'd killed himself and left a note explaining why he'd done what he did. He'd said he felt betrayed. It was Grace who showed Okika the blog post with pictures of the murder scene, the woman's braids uprooted from her head, scattered like feathers all over the room. 'He must have been so angry he was just throwing the hair anyhow,' Okika said. He couldn't understand that sort of anger that caused one to lose so much control that he'd murder a woman he loved. Or murder anyone, for that matter. Now, Grace looked at him and thought she could feel that sort of anger swooping down on him, in the cold that was emanating from his eyes.

She had met Okika the year after she started working at UNTH, almost seven years after she'd had her baby. Okika was not conventionally handsome, but there was an attractiveness to him that she had found impossible to ignore in the pictures he posted on the dating site that Grace had joined because her job left her little time to meet anyone. She liked that he described himself as God-fearing, looking to settle down and not afraid to do housework. A Nigerian man who liked to do housework? She'd asked him about it the day they met.

'I lived abroad alone for a while. I had to do it. Why stop just because one is married? Besides, whatever a woman can do, a man can do better.' He smiled. That first day, she had to lean in to hear his voice above the music playing in the restaurant she'd picked out. The music wasn't necessarily loud; Okika just spoke like someone who was used to whispering, the way men who were used to being listened to did. Working in a ward where women screamed in labour and screamed as they were giving birth, women who refused epidurals because they wanted to 'suffer like the Israelites' or 'like our mothers did', she was happy to be with someone who spoke in such soft tones. It was soothing. It was enough to make her think she could learn to love. And she did learn to love him, even if that love had nothing to do with sex. He was placid, like water, calm until stirred, and she had no intention of stirring him. She had fallen in love with the world he promised, even if not with the man himself. This was not a man to probe, to ask too many questions. She could settle down with him and that was as good as love, which she no longer believed in. It had become clear to both of them early enough that they wanted to be exclusive. In fact, the night after their first date, Grace had cancelled dates she had planned with two other men who seemed interesting, and she had taken her profile down. Yes, she was putting all her eggs in one basket, but if one was lucky enough to find the perfect basket for all of one's eggs, what use was there in putting them in different ones?

'I told you about my son,' Okika finally said. His voice was back to normal. Almost.

'I know and I'm sorry,' Grace said. But even as she said it, she wondered how Okika could have thought that her having a child and him having one were the same. He had always been oblivious to the fact that her life – that life for all women – was different from what it was for men. They had had an argument once when she had told him he could try speaking up because 'It is so bloody tiring having to lean in to hear you!' And he retorted in his wisp of a voice that no one was stopping her from speaking softly. 'The whole world is!' she shouted. A woman in her position couldn't afford to have a soft voice. She would be trampled all over. 'Think of all the women in positions of power you know,' she said. 'They boom!' she screeched in his ear.

'Sorry? No,' Okika said now. He turned and went into the bedroom. Grace did not follow immediately. She went to the medicine cabinet in the kitchen for some painkillers. Her shoes were killing her too, she noticed now. She flung them off her feet and then dragged herself to the bedroom. There, she found Okika throwing things hurriedly into a suitcase. His shirts. Trousers. When she tried to hold him, he shook her off and held his hands up in front of her as if to forestall an onslaught. She thought of a poem she read a long time ago about hands around a neck. It felt to her like something or someone had died. It was then that Grace began to cry.

Fourteen

New Lay Out, Enugu

2020

Somewhere in the room, a fly buzzed. Grace groaned and covered her ears with a pillow. She had mosquito netting on the windows; there should have been no way for insects to get in. Her body felt welded to the bed and she thought she would never get out of it. She had no idea where Okika had gone and she was too numb to panic. Besides, he would come back. He couldn't leave the house, leave her, leave their girls, this beautiful life they had built, and disappear. He probably just needed to clear his head. He would be back soon.

Nevertheless, she was grateful to have an entire day to herself without anyone in her way. Hopefully by Sunday, when the girls returned, Okika would be back and there would be no need for them to know anything of what had happened while they were gone. Okika would probably call, once he had a chance to cool down. She would apologize again; she'd make him see why she could not have told him. He must know what things were like for women in this country. She could not have made the same choice that he had made. Besides, none of it was her fault. Not the pregnancy, not the baby she was made to abandon and not not tell the man who wanted to marry her. He had to understand that she'd wanted a life where she could pretend the pregnancy and the abandonment had never happened, and the only way to do that was by cutting ties with her parents. *This shouldn't have to change things between us*, she wanted to say but his phone was switched off. If only she knew where he was, she'd go there and find him and bring him home. She'd tell him not to let her foolish mother ruin what they had. Grace dragged herself out of bed to get some more painkillers because the headache had returned. She rubbed her temples and tried to shake off the feeling of foreboding. Nothing good was likely to come from her mother digging all of this up. And since when had she become superstitious? Believing all that nonsense about a curse enough to come and torpedo Grace's orderly life? Couldn't she just have kicked Ben's parents out of her home? Got her own back for the humiliation they put her through when she and Grace had gone to tell them about the pregnancy. How small they had made Grace and her mother feel in their massive sitting room, which, when Grace now thought of it, wasn't as big as the one in Grace's present home. Life is turn by turn, she said to herself. A phrase her father had used often in the past and which had made Grace, as a child, think of life as a carousel on which you sat for a while but relinquished for someone else once your turn was over. She rubbed her temple some more, but it was futile. Her head still pounded. She went back to the room, drew the blinds and lay in bed. The clinic would have to do without her today. She had a manager after all. A coterie of staff: three midwives, two nurses, a youth corper doctor, a recent graduate whom Grace paid a better stipend than any hospital would have paid her, because Grace wanted to retain her after her mandatory service, and an older doctor who had retired from the government hospital and now worked part time for Grace. His hands were shaky and his eyesight going but young pregnant women were reassured by his age. He was the only man Grace employed (apart from her driver and gatemen) and the oldest because she had made a vow to herself that when she was able to, she would make sure as many young women as possible had access to financial independence. Grace believed that it levelled the playing field; it made it easier for women to have options. And she kept her promise of ensuring that they were well paid. There was no one there who needed their hand held. They could survive a day without her. In fact, if it wasn't that Grace enjoyed seeing the joy on the faces of the new parents, she could stay home and her clinic would run itself. The clinic store was stocked. Cartons of foodstuff and milk. She outsourced meal preparation to a caterer in Emene – breakfast, lunch and dinner, so that patients ate properly and for free. Her dispensary fed them a diet of prenatal vitamins and iron tablets. Her pregnant women always looked well, their babies born healthy.

Her head hurt still. She and Okika had never had a falling out so bad that he'd slept outside their home. Not even when he'd disagreed with the baby business. And he had been vehement in his disagreement. 'It seems obscene, exchanging babies for money.'

'But a huge chunk of the money goes to the mothers who don't want them, and the babies go to homes where they *are* wanted.'

'Still, babe. It feels too much like trading. I don't want you to do it.' Then he thought better of it and said, 'I'd rather you didn't.'

Grace, who had had enough in her youth of people telling her what to do, clung on to that and the argument spiralled and soon it was no longer about the clinic or about the babies but about control. Yet, after all that, they had still shared a bed that night, sleeping not with their faces towards one other as they mostly did but turning away, their backs in opposite directions. The next morning, there had been a bit of coolness, which even their then five-year-old twins had noticed, but by the time they both came home from work, they were back to normal. Okika still did not like the idea of the baby business, but he never raised it again. Grace knew only because whenever she began to talk about a placement, he always found a way to change the subject.

She didn't want to think about Okika now. Her headache had eased somewhat, but the fly was still buzzing somewhere in the room. She got up and went outside. As she walked towards her car, her driver materialized from the gateman's station. She waved him away. She did not often drive herself, but today she could not abide anyone else with her in the car, even if it was Odiuko who did not speak unless she spoke to him. She eased herself behind the steering wheel, adjusted the setting and drove with no destination in mind. In her head, images of that night played out like a scene in a film.

Fifteen

New Haven, Enugu

1994

Grace's baby came before dawn, when night still lingered. She had woken up to a dampness in her bed, and some cramping around ten o'clock. When the pain worsened, she crawled into her parents' bedroom and shook her mother awake. In the last month of Grace's pregnancy, her mother had taken temporary leave from work. 'When the pains start, no matter what time it is, call me.' Her mother sprang up, the squeaking of the bed not even waking Grace's father.

'Dibe ya, bear it. Don't shout ooo, even if the pain grows sharp teeth and bites you, do not make a single sound,' she reminded Grace, whispering furiously. In the kitchen, she flipped on the light switch. 'Thank God there's power today,' she said. She unrolled the mat that she'd bought for the delivery on the floor, a sliver of space between the fridge and the sink. Their kitchen backed onto the one of the family next door, but at that time of night, nobody was likely to be in theirs. However, it wasn't so late that everyone would have gone to bed. She gave Grace a chewing stick to bite down on for the pain. 'We don't want the neighbourhood hearing,' she said. Not after they had been successful in hiding the pregnancy. It was fortunate, her mother said, that Grace was not slim. No one noticed the extra weight she had been carrying unless they looked at her properly. And to look that properly, they would have to have been searching. And to have been searching, they would have heard rumours. But no one knew of the pregnancy except Grace, her parents and Ben's family. And Ben's family wanted nothing at all to do with it, so it was not likely that they would tell anyone. 'It's a man's world,' Grace's mother told her as Grace clenched her teeth against the pain that was a furnace inside of her. 'You're here suffering. The young man responsible for it isn't even thinking of you. He's living his life. Nothing. Nothing has changed for him.' Her mother sounded regretful. While Grace had to stop school and hide inside her house for the last three months of the pregnancy, while her parents told neighbours and guests that she had a bad case of typhoid fever, Ben's life remained untouched.

'Once a child has eaten that which is keeping him awake, he goes to bed. Nwata lie ife o na-amulu anya, o laluo ula,' her mother said as she caught her daughter's eye. Grace wasn't in the mood for proverbs. All she wanted was for the woman to still the pain which no longer paused for Grace to recover before hitting her again.

'I want to push,' Grace said. Her mother helped her down on the mat, pushed down on her stomach with one hand and inserted another into her. When had she put on gloves, Grace wondered.

'Don't push until I ask you to.' Grace nodded. 'Baby is crowning. Not long now.'

★ ★ ★

The baby was perfect. After letting out her first cry, her mouth formed a permanent pout as if she was posing for a photograph. Grace took her all in. She didn't care if the neighbours heard the cry, didn't care how her parents would explain it away, if they did; she was in awe of her baby. What a miracle she was, Grace thought. Every part of her. The tiny fingers, the nose already like Ben's, the head full of fine, dark hair. Grace held the baby close to her own body, amazed that such perfection had come out of her. Her mother pried the baby from Grace, and then disappeared into the house with her. She returned and stayed with Grace until she delivered the placenta. Grace felt as if someone had taken an axe to her insides, hacking and gouging out and rearranging everything. Her mother cleaned up around her with a quiet efficiency, removing every evidence of a birth. She would cut up the mat and throw it away later. She helped Grace up, into the shower, into another nightgown and into Grace's own bed. She handed Grace two Panadol tablets. Grace did everything she was asked to do. She'd imagined that if she obeyed, her baby would be restored to her. She had gone to bed a child, and now she was a mother. Her stomach cramped still, and the Panadol didn't seem to help. Her mother returned about half an hour later with a steaming bowl of omugwo soup. 'Sit up and eat.' She handed the tray of food to Grace. The soup burned Grace's tongue. It was fire going down her throat and into the pit of her stomach. Not once did Grace whimper. She ate until there was nothing left in the bowl. 'It will make the cramps worse, but it will make them stop quicker. It will help you heal,' her mother said. Grace drank the glass of water held out to her. Sweat beads formed on her forehead from the pepper and the heat and the childbirth. She wanted her baby, but her mother now held the infant, dressed in a hideous, egg-coloured onesie Grace had never seen, and would not relinquish her. Her father stood at the door of her bedroom and her parents whispered about what to do with her, as if they had not already decided in all the time they knew of their daughter's pregnancy that there could be only one outcome. Her mother fed the baby infant formula siphoned from the hospital where she worked while Grace watched, the pain in her heart stronger than the pain of labour and childbirth.

Grace was forbidden from naming her child. She was called Baby or the baby. Grace's father never held Baby. Not once. And Grace herself wasn't allowed to until just under forty-five hours old, when Baby was handed to her and she was asked to 'take care of it'. Her mother said a quiet prayer over the crying infant before handing her over to Grace. Baby had stopped crying. 'You know what to do.'

The neighbourhood was asleep, and it was easy for her to sneak out of the compound. It was like an out-of-body experience, Grace plodding along, the baby tucked under her arm like a bundle of clothes. It felt to her as if her insides had been rearranged by the delivery. Her mother's soup appeared to have helped, as the intensity of the cramps and their frequency had lessened after a day. She prayed that the street would be as deserted as it always was at that time of the night. Prayed that a miracle would change her parents' minds. Prayed for strength that would allow her to run with her baby until they'd left New Haven behind, left Enugu behind, toppled together off the edge of the world. Baby was still new, but Grace already knew that she was the most beautiful thing she had ever seen.

Sixteen

Trans-Ekulu, Enugu

2020

Grace had always found driving therapeutic, but right now it wasn't helping to distract her from the memories and regrets crowding her mind. Grace wished she had a photo or had taken a lock of the baby's hair, something that might help with the loss she still felt inside. It was true what they said about grief, she thought. It came in waves, and this wave, precipitated by her mother's reappearance, was enough to knock her out. Her twins were now slightly older, by a few months, than she had been when she became pregnant. She could not even imagine her girls, whom she considered children still, although they were old enough to wear make-up, having the kind of relationship she had had with Ben. They were smarter than she was at their age, for one, and part of that had to do with her. She talked to them regularly about hormones, boys and sex. They would not make her mistake. And if they did, she knew they trusted her enough to come to her. She did not want them to be blindsided like she was. How naïve she had been and how easy it had been for Ben to manipulate her. It was only as an adult that it occurred to Grace that Ben had planned the whole thing. He had intended to have his way with her. The water he poured on her was no accident, nor was getting her into bed. He must have known that she could get pregnant, although it did not, as incredible as it seemed now, occur to her then. All the nonsense she had believed. Ben (via his brother) had said he couldn't use a condom because it could slide up Grace's vagina and make her stomach swell. All that rubbish she'd swallowed about saline water blocking off a pregnancy. They had not even discussed the possibility of it, did not take any of the precautions that they could have.

Ben hadn't deserved to have a good life. Her parents hadn't either. She drove past WTC primary school and thought of the couple who had come from Owerri to get a baby from her. They said a teacher at WTC had told them about Grace. They had been married for close to five years and had been excited at the first meeting when they came to place an order for a baby born within six to nine months from then. They had always wanted a child, they said, and after years of fruitless IVF (which 'did nothing but make me add weight,' the woman said) and two years of surrogacies that did not work either, they had decided to go a different route. Their IVF journey had taken them on multiple flights to India. 'Bloody waste of money,' the man said, fingering the leather clutch wallet he'd dropped on the table before him. A friend who knew of their struggles had told them of Grace and how she could help them. Grace did not advertise, except for her regular maternity services, but people who needed to know of the extra service she provided always got to know, via word of mouth. It was like an exclusive club, and she liked to keep it that way. She wanted her clientele to know that whichever baby they got from her would never, ever find a way back to the birth parents. It would be years before she would hear of a Doctor Hicks, in some village in Georgia – somewhere beginning with a 'Mac' and ending with a 'ville' that she could never remember whenever she tried to retell the story – who did the same in the 1950s and 60s. Grace would sit, her eyes glued to the screen, watching the American TV documentary about this man who sold babies for a thousand dollars to desperate parents, and Grace would think that it did not matter where or when: humans are invariably the same. She would also tell herself that while the mothers of the 'Hicks babies' were told that their babies had died or that the abortions some of them had come for had been completed while they were sedated, the pregnant women who came to her always knew the deal and always left with money. That, after all, was why they came. Like Ifeatu always said, she helped women who would have been lost without her. The couple from Owerri had been excited when they came to take the baby, talking over each other about who would be the child's favourite parent, giggling like young people who had just discovered love. Yet, two weeks later, they had returned the infant because the woman said she found it difficult to love a child that had not come from her own womb. 'I've tried,' she said. She looked like she was in pain – not an emotional ache in her heart but a physical one.

'You can't just return her. She's not a . . . a . . .' Grace tried to think of something anyone could buy and return, but no store would take anything back after it had been bought. At least, not in Enugu. And no matter that money exchanged hands, Grace did not consider what she did to be trading. She was a compassionate woman who helped give babies, who would otherwise have had no chance, good, loving homes. And in so doing, she was giving others who wanted to raise children a chance to do so. Those who came to her for babies *wanted* those babies. But this couple no longer wanted the child they had *oohed* and *aahed* over and taken into their home. 'I tried,' the woman said again, something hard entering her voice. Like a pebble. Or maybe a piece of metal. Something forged in a fire. 'I can't come and kill myself because of somebody else's child, biko.' Grace fumed inside and said to herself: *But you did say it killed you not to have a child, you foolish woman. Now, it's you can't 'come and kill yourself' over somebody else's child'?* Grace sighed and cracked her knuckles. 'What do you want me to do? Sometimes, these things, even for a biological mother, take time. I know a woman who didn't even want to hold the baby she had given birth to for many months.' She didn't know any such woman, but she had read enough medical journals to know that such women existed. Grace looked from the wife to the husband. She wished she could smoke but she hadn't smoked in years. And even if she hadn't, she couldn't very well smoke in front of clients. Former clients. Anyone. It would ruin her reputation. No woman who wanted to be taken seriously smoked. Certainly not where it could be witnessed. The woman was furiously shaking her head like an agitated dog and talking over Grace. She thought that the years of childlessness would make it easy for her to love any child, but she couldn't. She turned to her husband as if seeking support. He did not say a word. Grace was happy to see that he at least had the common sense to look embarrassed. 'I look at this child and she's a total stranger to me,' the woman said, the thing in her voice becoming harder. It sounded like she was now spitting out shrapnel, something from an explosion. 'Lie-lie, I can't keep this baby ooo.' Her husband had told her the same thing, told her that maybe she needed more time with the infant, that he was not comfortable returning a child they had taken as theirs, a child they had named, set up a nursery for – but her mind was made up. She did not care that it could be bad karma for her, she did not care if she never had any child, she did not care what anyone thought of her. She would not swallow phlegm out of embarrassment. Lie-lie. The baby gurgled through all of this, even though the woman held the infant away from her, turned to face Grace rather than to face the woman who had been her mother for a short while. Grace had not returned the money they had paid – part of which had already gone to the twenty-one-year-old university student who'd birthed the child. Grace had ended up making a huge profit when another couple on her list picked up the baby straight away. Grace had had to make a new birth certificate with new names and a new date of birth. From then on, she made her customers sign what she called 'forever parents' waivers that stipulated that they would never return the babies they took home. If the baby woke up one day with an extra eye, or a sixth toe, they were not to involve Grace or her clinic. 'These are flesh-and-blood humans,' she complained to Okika later. Imagine what would have happened had she not had a couple who were not precious about having a daughter or a son. They were just happy with a child and had even invited Grace to the naming ceremony of their baby held in the reception hall of a posh hotel where the new baby was bounced from knee to knee and guests exclaimed that she was such a healthy size for her age. If any of the guests gorging themselves on fried rice and salad suspected anything, they kept it to themselves and congratulated the parents as sensible people did.

Grace became upset all over again, just remembering the incident with the couple, which did not help her mood. Maybe she should drive to Shoprite, get some of that expensive Toblerone chocolate the girls liked. She drove along Ogui Road, headed towards Abakaliki Road, but she hadn't even stopped at Shoprite. It was as if the car had its own mind and, despite what her head and heart were telling her, it was determined to have its own way. She drove along Ezechime Street and found herself stopping at the address beside Trans-Ekulu Secondary School that she could not even remember memorizing. Grace had not intended to drive to her parents' house. Both her flesh and spirit were unwilling to face the ghosts of her past. When her mother had left their address, on a sheet of paper, Grace had barely looked at it. And yet now here she was, looking at a pink duplex with a fence around it. There was no gateman, but the gate was open. To the right was a bungalow, painted a more sensible maroon. In its front yard, a young boy played football by himself. He waved at her. Grace waved back. She wondered whose idea it was to paint a house in Enugu pink. She would have chosen a colour that would hide the inevitable dirt from the unforgiving harmattan dust. The rainy season was mild but the house was still coated in grime. Yet, she could imagine her parents being very proud of it. It was a far cry from the flats she had lived in as a child with narrow verandas and no green spaces. Here were trees, high and weighed down with fruit. An oasis in the middle of a city that was – despite its tree-lined streets – becoming a concrete jungle. She imagined growing up here, standing under the cashew tree, eating a plump yellow or red cashew in the sun. Beside the gate, hedges of ixoras and hibiscus flowers bloomed, heavy with life. Over the steel balustrade of balcony facing the front yard, pink and crimson bougainvillea cascaded dramatically. Inside the front yard itself were other flowers and plants Grace did not recognize. A paradise of colours: bright pinks and yellows and purples and blues. She wondered whose handiwork it was. Which of her parents loved gardening? She could not imagine. Neither had done it when she was young. Where would they have? The places they had lived in then had cemented front yards on which children played and scraped their knees. How little she knew of her parents. Their likes, their dislikes, their hobbies. She had not expected all this aggressive shine and beauty and life. It seemed like a house that ought to belong to someone else, not the parents she remembered who had no hobbies she could recall. Had her mother ever sat down after work to read or knit or do anything that seemed like leisure? No. Her father? No. The most they read was the daily newspaper. She parked in the driveway and, as she walked to the front door, she saw a curtain move. Her mother held the door open before she could ring the bell.

'I knew you'd come,' her mother said and stood aside to let Grace in. She bellowed inside for Grace's father,

her voice oddly deeper than it had been when Grace was a child. 'Grace is here!' The house smelled of ofe okwuru and Grace remembered how she loved her mother's soup. She'd always looked forward to Saturday afternoons when her mother made eba and okra, her favourite childhood dish. Inside the house, Grace felt as if she was in a time warp. On the walls were the same pictures of Grace and her parents that had been on the walls when she lived with them. It was as if life had stopped the year before Grace got pregnant, which was the last time they took a family portrait. They had dressed up and gone to Captain Jo, the photographer in Uwani who was all the rage back then. People said he was the official photographer of the state Governor and, when Grace asked him if it was true, he had not denied it. In the pictures, it was easy to see Grace's awe in her eyes and the reverence in her half smile. In one, she was sitting with her parents standing on either side of her, a hand each on her shoulder, like guardian angels. All three were in clothes made of identical wax material. In a second one, they were all lying on the floor, elbows propped, heads lifted, gazing intently into the camera. Grace remembered that her father had joked afterwards that for the price of the pictures, they could have built an entire block of flats. It had been like an outing to a different life. Everyone in Enugu who could afford it wanted their pictures taken by Captain Jo, who had trained abroad, and gave everyone a radiant gloss. Grace's family had made a day of it, filled with the goodness of having just had their photos taken, and her mother had insisted on all of them going to Genesis for spring rolls with hot sauce. Grace had not thought of that day in years and now it shocked her to remember it, to remember how happy they were, because for so long her memory of childhood was one long period of misery. She remembered her father kissing her mother on the lips at Genesis and how embarrassed Grace had been to see them openly affectionate, and in public.

'Papa Grace! Grace is here!' her mother shouted. She sounded breathless, as if she'd been in the middle of a marathon. When her father shuffled out of the room, holding the loosened end of the wrapper around his waist in one hand, Grace wanted both to fold him in her arms and to run away at the same time. Her father looked so old, so frail, that anyone could have mistaken him for a man in his nineties. Maybe her mother saw something in Grace's eyes because she said, 'Your father is sick. He's been sick for a few years now and then COVID hit him, but God's been faithful. He's here and you're here.' Her mother sounded like she was ready to burst into song. Or into tears. Grace hoped she would do neither even as she, Grace, started to cry.

Seventeen

Trans-Ekulu, Enugu

2020

Grace thought of Baby crying that night, as if she knew what was going to happen to her, and she wondered why she had come to her parents' house now. She thought of how difficult it had been to let go. She had often wondered how differently things would have turned out had, back then, there been a place like the clinic she herself ran now. If it would have been easier to give Baby up, knowing she was going to go to a wealthy home where she was desperately wanted. So desperately wanted that the new parents were willing to pay lots of money for her. The two things all her clients had in common were their wealth and their desperation. Both made for good homes for the children she handed over. And both made it worthwhile. Knowing that the children were going to have better lives than they would have otherwise. She did not keep in touch with a lot of the parents except those who became repeat customers – and those were few. People preferred to come from out of town, but Grace was known for her discretion. Her clients trusted her to keep their secret. It was partly what they paid for. They could get a better deal by adopting but, once you adopted, it was legal, there were paper trails and you could not pretend to the world that the baby was biologically yours. Grace knew of at least two clients who had left the country for many months and 'returned' with a baby. Not even their parents knew the truth of the 'pregnancies'. There were others who ran businesses like Grace's, but Grace was diligent. And she was exclusive. She made early-morning and late-night drop-offs if needed. She met clients wherever they wanted to be met, spreading joy and saving marriages from the interference of in-laws wondering why there was no baby yet, one child at a time. If her own Baby had had the same kind of chance she was offering other babies, it would have made days like today more bearable for Grace. Her clients were the sort who could afford to send their children to elite private schools, hire tutors and spend holidays abroad. Those children were *made*. Ajebo children who had bread and butter for breakfast and not the yam and palm oil staple she had sometimes relied on. Grace doubted that Baby had survived. If she had, would the papers not have mentioned the finding of an infant? They always ran stories of abandoned babies found by some passer-by, often accompanied by grainy pictures. But there was nothing in the papers about a found baby (her mother had scoured newspapers for news for weeks after). Grace had hoped that there would be, so that she could clip the picture. If someone found her dead, they might have got rid of the body, thrown it into the garbage. On good days, she preferred to think that Baby had simply vanished, leaving nothing of her short stay behind. On bad days, Grace imagined that a ritualist had picked her up and chopped off her limbs for some money-making ceremony. Today was a bad day and Grace could not stop the tears from rolling down.

Grace could hear her mother tell her to sit down, as if Grace was a guest she was eager to impress. Touching her elbow like an usher at church to show her to her seat. All the chairs were covered in pink velvet. Grace had come without meaning to. She could not see through the tears that had, unbidden, misted her eyes. Her heart felt like a heavy weight was placed on it and it was crushing her, but the more she cried, the more the pressure on her heart released itself, so she allowed the tears to flow.

Grace stood rooted near the sofa while her father ambled towards her, his walking stick making a *tap tap tap* sound on the linoleum floor. When he came close enough, he put the stick under one arm and spread out his arms. Grace fell into his embrace, all the anger she thought she felt dissipating. She was not sure if she imagined that he smelled of the aftershave he used in her childhood, but the scent was strong, entering her nose. 'Daddy,' she said, feeling how bony her father had become. It was like hugging a bird and she worried that she might break something. 'Daddy,' she said again, unable to say more, releasing her hold on him a little bit. Her father disentangled himself from her. 'COVID,' he said. He put out a bony hand and touched her cheek. Grace held the hand to her cheek, enjoying its warmth. 'Let's sit,' he said. Leading her by the hand like a child, he sat her on the same sofa on which he sat. He had caught COVID in March, he said, and three months later was still dealing with the complications. 'I got all the symptoms. Fever. Cough. Low oxygen. Rashes. I keep telling your mother I should play the lottery. Or maybe she should, because she never caught it. Or if she did, she was asymptomatic.' He chuckled but Grace could not laugh.

'We almost lost him,' her mother said. The words hit Grace like an accusation. Her father could have died and she would never have known. But hadn't she spent years pretending they were dead? She tried to call up the anger that had made her tell them to stay away from her life, but she could not. Even as she drove down today, she had been angry. So where was that anger now? It was as if seeing her father in the flesh, being in her parents' new house, smelling the familiar okra soup, gathered up all her memories, sifted them. The heavier ones, the chunky ones that were heavy enough to break apart the family, were taken and hurled away. She was a kid again, the only child of parents who doted on her. Her parents took her out often. To interesting places. The zoo, to Polo Park when it was still a park to walk around. No one else she knew lived like that. Her friends' parents thought it a waste of time to go to the zoo. 'To see what?' Amaka, her best friend, had mimicked her mother, asking her why she wanted to go to the zoo. 'The only animals I want to see are the ones on my plate ready to be eaten,' Amaka's mother had said. Grace hadn't seen Amaka since they left elementary school. 'You're so lucky, Grace,' Amaka had told her. How uncomplicated and beautiful her life had been.

Grace closed her eyes and imagined that she was fifteen again, only this time there was no Ben. No pregnancy. Just her and her parents in a house on Trans-Ekulu that smelled so familiar to her even though she had never been in it before. Why had it all gone so terribly wrong? Was it because once she entered secondary school, her parents' doting on her had manifested itself as prying? Her mother especially. Wanting to know where she was, who she was with, as if she was still a child. That was why Ben calling her a baby had had such an effect on her, why she had been so determined to show that she wasn't one. It had not helped that, unlike at elementary school where she'd had many friends, she'd barely had any in secondary school. All of her friends had gone to different schools and she'd ended up in a school where she faded into the walls. Ben had made her feel like she was *something*. She looked around the house, amused by the tackiness of her parents' style. Had it always been so? She could not tell. The walls of the sitting room were painted pink. There were pink curtains and a coffee table with a red top that was so light it could be pink. All that pink made it seem like a giant doll house.

'You never gave us a chance to say thank you for all this,' her father said, his voice small and tired. He waved his hands over the chairs, the colour TV in a corner, the walls.

'If not for your money,' her mother said, 'things would have been hard for us. Very hard. Your father's hospital bill alone would have wiped us out.' Her father had lost so much weight that Grace was sure that she could lift him up as easily as she lifted the new babies born in her clinic, carrying them to be weighed.

'You'll stay and eat? I'm making ofe okwuru, your favourite,' her mother said as if Grace had told them she was coming.

Her father answered before Grace could. 'Of course she will. You will, won't you?'

Her mother began to talk about the neighbours who lived to the right of them. A single mother. Young.

Beautiful. Three rambunctious children. They loved her okra too. The eldest, Anuli, was a star athlete at her school. Grace's mother's voice dripped with pride, like a grandmother talking about her high-achieving grandchildren. The middle son, Ndu, wanted to be a pilot. 'Only twelve years old and so focused. I've been teaching him how to cook. The youngest boy, Oku, keeps your father on his toes. He calls him GrumpPa.' Grace's mother laughed, her laughter grating on Grace, who was suddenly angry again. The fury that she thought had left her came slithering back in, filling every part of her like a multitude of worms. She wanted to throw up. Her parents playing happy families with a neighbour and her children when they had made her get rid of their own grandchild. Acting as if Grace had just popped out to say hello to a friend and re-turned instead of being away from them for years and years. She sprang up from her chair. The tears had long stopped rolling.

'I don't know why I came. I shouldn't have.' Grace interrupted her mother who was in the middle of some anecdote about Anuli and her brothers.

'Grace, please don't go. We want to talk. We have to,' her father said. The 'please' took Grace by surprise. Growing up, it was clear to her that there were things parents did not do. They didn't say *please, thank you, sorry* or *I love you*. They expressed it in other ways, but they never said it. When she fetched the slippers her parents asked her to from their room, they praised her for being a good girl. When her parents were feeling especially affectionate, Grace got a pat on the head or a special treat. And when her parents were sorry? That never happened because parents were never wrong. Grace had thought it normal. It would have been laughable to anyone she knew back then that parents might apologize to their children. It was not how she was raising her children. She apologized to them, told them she loved them. Okika was the same. It was one of the many things on which they had agreed. Their children had to be comfortable enough with them to talk to them. Okika told her of how his family's driver had taught him to drive at twelve, teaching him in a field far away from their house, away from the prying eyes of his parents and siblings. Grace dragged her mind away from Okika. 'Sit down, please, my daughter.' The second 'please' propelled Grace into the chair nearest to her. The cushion was surprisingly thick; it was like sitting on a brick. The anger that found its way back was a furnace burning her up. She understood now what it meant to 'boil with anger'. She had read somewhere that slapping a chicken several times could cook it. She was sure her rage could cook an entire goat. Or a cow even.

'There are things we need to talk about, Grace.'

'If it's about Ben and his parents, I don't want to hear it,' Grace said. *And if it's about these wonderful grandchildren you've adopted next door, you can save it as well*, she added in her mind.

'So why have you come?' her mother asked, sounding almost combative. Grace wanted to tell her that she had no right to raise her voice at her. But she said nothing. She had no response. Why had she come? She thought now that it was curiosity. Having seen her mother, she'd wanted to see her father too. She admitted to herself that even through the fog of a headache the day before, she had wondered about her parents, about this house on Trans-Ekulu she hadn't even known they'd bought. She'd wanted to see it for herself and, now she had, she was patting herself on the back for being able to provide all this for them. It was bigger than any flat they'd lived in while she was growing up and, tacky furnishing aside, it was beautiful. From where she was sitting, Grace could see into the open kitchen, dark brown cupboards lining its wall. She knew if she went in there, there'd be a fridge humming silently in a corner, probably something sleek and modern, not any of the bulky boxes they'd used more as cupboards than as fridges in her childhood. One even had a lock attached to it by the local carpenter because one of Grace's father's good friends at the time, a man with a goatee who used to tell Grace horror stories to her mother's annoyance, used to feel so much at home that he'd walk in and go to the fridge for whatever he needed. The day after he ate all four of the eggs Grace's mother had been saving for her own breakfast, she had the lock installed. It was easier than telling him to behave, but the relationship between Grace's father and the man had cooled after that.

'I don't want to talk about Ben and his family,' Grace said again. She opened and closed her purse, feeling like that teenager who was dragged to Ben's house by her mother. 'Since when are you best friends with them, anyway?' she asked, throwing the question at her mother who was still standing by the door as if she was guarding it. The hem of her long, flowing boubou swept the floor. 'Have you forgotten what they did to you?' For years, it had haunted Grace that her mother had allowed anyone to speak to her the way Ben's mother had and that her mother had taken it because Ben's family was wealthier. Many people were subservient in the presence of wealth. Her mother moved from the door to sit across from Grace.

'The stench of that humiliation is still in my nose,' she said quietly, suddenly sounding old and tired, and Grace felt a momentary guilt for asking. She remembered how difficult it had been for her mother to unglue herself from the chair at Ben's parents'. Throughout their journey home her mother had walked as if someone had placed a basin of pineapples on her back, so stooped was she. 'What was I to do, Grace? Tell me.' The neckline of her mother's boubou was thick with sweat although it had started to rain outside and the weather had cooled considerably. It seemed as if her mother had physically made the trek back to Ben's house in New Haven in the moment since Grace reminded her of the shame of that visit. She took a newspaper from the centre table and began to fan herself, repeating the same question, her voice breaking so that Grace feared that she might cry. 'What was I to do, Grace?'

'I was a child. I needed you to look after me. Both of you.'

I needed you to love me.

Eighteen

Trans-Ekulu, Enugu

2020

We love what we remember most. A teacher said that once to Grace's class, and one bright student had countered, saying maybe it was the opposite. 'Maybe we remember what we love most.' The teacher had asked the class to reflect on it and write an essay on whichever of the two statements they thought made better sense. Grace was twelve and, like most of her classmates, eager to please the teacher. Without giving it further thought she had taken the teacher's side. Over the years, whenever Grace remembered it (which was very often, because that student had ended up becoming a journalist and was on Arise TV every day), she thought that her classmate was right. She had spent years not remembering her parents, but she was sure that underneath the anger and the not-remembering was love. For years she had given them a monthly allowance, raising it as her circumstances improved. It wasn't forced on her. There was a satisfaction and joy beyond merely fulfilling a duty. Had she never given her parents a cent, they never would have come demanding it. And yet, without thinking of them or remembering them most of the time, she made the monthly transfer. On the first of every month, without fail. Love, she was convinced, had nothing to do with proximity or memory or fondness or any of the other things she had often heard spoken of when people spoke of love. It was instinct. The opposite of love wasn't hate, either, because she both loved and hated her parents. One was instinctive, the other was a choice. And she wasn't indifferent to her parents – otherwise she wouldn't have cared how they lived or be in this house with them now, in this sitting room with its garish pink covers. It wasn't indifference that brought her here, her love for them and her hatred for them mixing in her head and threatening to drive her mad. If she was indifferent to them, they would have remained dead. If she had made the cut permanent, not giving her parents any reason to believe that she cared for them at all, her mother would never have come to her house and turned Grace's life upside down. When Okika returned, she would make him forgive her. She would make him see that she could not have told him about her past and that the past did not matter. What mattered was their present; why let the past spoil it?

'You know, my husband's left the house and I have no idea where he is. You . . .' Grace said, looking not at her mother, but at a point above her head, the smell of the goat and okra from the kitchen wafting into her nose and distracting her so that she forgot what she was about to say and left it hanging. It was not her mother who responded but her father who said he was sorry.

'He'll come back.' His brittle, flat voice did not carry any weight of conviction.

Grace snapped. 'What do you know about him? You've never even met him. He thinks . . . he thought you were dead. Both of you. It was what I told him.' Grace held eyes with her father as she said this. The joy that she got from seeing him flinch was momentary. It was like kicking someone who was already down. Her father looked like an odd species of bird. His nose, curved like a beak, his head now bald, his cheeks sunken, his neck thin. His shoulders with their sharp edges like sloping wings.

'Don't talk to your father like that.' Her mother had found her voice. She had always been the one to come to her husband's defense. Grace thought now that she and her mother were more alike than she'd believed. They were both attracted to men who did not say much. Men who occupied very little space. 'You keep blaming us, but what would you do if your daughters – it's daughters you have, right? What if they brought home pregnancies at the age you did? Would you pat them on the head and say "well done"? Go out and get pregnant again?' Her mother hissed, got up and went to the kitchen to turn off the flame under the soup.

Grace stood up again and said to her mother's retreating back that her children would never get pregnant before they were ready, because she talked to them. 'They know how people get pregnant. The only time I asked you, you told me some bullshit!' Grace was shouting now. When her mother came back in from the kitchen, she stood in front of Grace. She was happy Grace had come. She'd be pleased if Grace stayed for food. But she had almost lost her husband, and if all Grace had come to do was to disrespect them, then she should go.

'The okra plant never grows taller than its planter. You

may be grown and wealthy, but we are still your parents. If you cannot respect us, then please go. It's a painful thing to lose a child, but I will not say sorry for trying to save you all those years ago. Do you know what keeping that baby would have done to you? You think you would have finished school? Found a husband? Managed to build a family? Have this clinic that you have? A baby at that age would have been the end of you.'

'You could have helped. I was a child. I was a child, Mother.' Grace was holding back the tears which moistened her voice. She would not cry or whine like a toddler.

'What if I didn't want to help? I'd raised you. You think I wanted to raise another baby? I was working. I had my own life. You know what that would have done to your name – to our name – had anyone found out? Once Ben's family wanted nothing to do with it, my hands were tied. You can't pretend not to know that! How would you have moved on, Grace? Tell me.' She was shouting, spittle flying out of her mouth, flying into the air and disappearing. As if the speaking had worn her out, Grace's mother slowly dropped into a chair. She held her head in her hands and Grace was shocked to see that her mother was crying, her shoulders heaving. Her father scooted closer to his wife and began to rub her back as if she were a child needing consolation, the way her mother used to comfort Grace. Her father did not once look at her. Not even when he began to speak, his voice stretching and stretching, covering every bit of the house like something carried by the wind.

Nineteen

Trans-Ekulu, Enugu

2020

The night Grace left with the baby, her mother had followed her at a distance like a ghost. She waited until Grace had walked out the front door into the street to walk behind her. She followed Grace as she walked down Chime Avenue, turned left past the pharmacy, then right into Edward Nnaji Street towards New Haven Primary School. She watched Grace wait for a car to pass before crossing over and turning right into Nzimiro Street, which was fairly deserted.

'She didn't want you to know,' her father said now. Grace felt tears rising. She cleared her throat. Her mother had followed her, hiding in the shadows, because what kind of a mother would let her child go through that alone? 'We couldn't have let you,' her father said. The tears rushed behind Grace's eyes, prickly and hot. If she cried now, she thought, it would scald her. 'You remember that when you came home, your mother wasn't there?'

Grace nodded. She remembered now, although she hadn't thought anything of it then. She had been so wrapped up in her own sorrow that her mother's absence at that time of the night had barely even registered. She had felt devoid of flesh, just a bag of clacking bones walking home with empty arms where a baby had lain, her stomach still flaccid from birth. The twenty minutes it had taken her to walk there and back had seemed like twenty hours. She remembered that she had gone straight to her room and lain on her bed, the pillow that had been Baby's bed bunched under her nose. She had tried and tried to extract the smell of Baby from it, but the pillow just smelled of detergent. She had prayed that the world would end or that she would die so that she did not have to wake up in the morning to a world where Baby was not with her. A single tear burned its way down her cheek. She wiped it away.

Her mother had stayed back, praying and waiting in the shadows until the baby was picked up. She would have slept there if it had meant doing so. 'She wanted to make sure Baby was safe,' her father went on. 'You should have seen her when she came back. I have never seen her look so broken before.' Her mother had watched as a couple walked towards the baby, watched as they carried her. That night, she dreamed, Grace's mother did, of the baby being snatched by a pack of wild dogs. The relief of having her taken was replaced by the worry that they might be evil people, that in trying to save one child, she and Grace's father had condemned the other to a tortuous death. She could not sleep well for days. She went to the neighbourhood where Baby was left and walked around, hoping to catch sight of her being pushed around in a pram, getting the life that a proper family could give her.

'And did she? Did you?' Grace whispered. Her body felt strange, as if she had malaria. She felt both cold and hot at the same time. Her mother shook her head no. Grace wrapped her arms around herself to shield her from the chill that had replaced the burning heat she'd had before and started rocking herself on the chair, back and forth, back and forth. Her head was full of things she wanted to say but the words were moving so fast she could not make them stop long enough to escape her lips, so when she opened her mouth, the only thing that came out sounded like a cross between a moan and a cough.

Outside, the rain that had started earlier was increasing in intensity, battering the windows so that it felt as if someone was throwing fistfuls of pebbles at them. If Grace were home, if her weekend had gone as planned, she and Okika would have been in bed drinking cocoa and watching TV like kids. And once the rain stopped, she would have gone outside to her backyard to inhale the scent of the earth. There was a word for it but she could never recall it. When she was a child and they lived in a flat in New Haven with multiple children around her age, they'd all run outside to play at the first sound of rain. Sometimes, the parents let them. Often, they were scolded back inside, parents asking, 'Do you want to catch pneumonia and die? Come out of the rain!' It took Grace until nursing school to learn that pneumonia was caused by a virus. How come her mother hadn't learned that?

An apparition appeared in the sitting room, drenched by the rain. A small boy of about ten or eleven, wearing tan shorts that blended with his skin and a T-shirt that said 'Fantastic'. He was clutching a paper bag dripping water on the tiled floor. He greeted Grace's parents and Grace herself. 'This is Lucky, who lives with us and helps us out.' Grace nodded in greeting at the boy, wiping her eyes furiously. The boy looked alarmed to see this grown-up with tears in her eyes. He kept staring at her until Grace's father asked him to get a rag to mop the floor that he was dripping water on, his voice soft.

'Get out of those clothes before you flood the house.'

'Yes, Daddy.'

Grace felt a momentary envy at their easy familiarity. She tried, without success, to remember how old she was when her father made her mop the entire house because she had committed the unforgivable sin of trailing water into the sitting room. She couldn't have been more than eight, but she had answered the call of the other neighbourhood children to come outside and play in the rain, forgetting that it had been forbidden her that day. Her father had woken up from his Sunday afternoon nap to notice that she was gone. He called her back inside, scolded her and asked to get a rag to mop not just the bit where she had dripped water but the entire house, including the toilet. She couldn't have done a good job because she remembered her father mopping after she'd finished. Her arms hurt from all the cleaning up and, when she'd told her father, he'd told her to remember how it hurt to disobey one's parents. Grace would never discipline her children that way, with such heavy hands. Her parents' heavy hands had considerably weakened now. Maybe age had mellowed them.

Grace felt silly for that second of jealousy. She ought to be happy that her parents treated him like family. She knew people who treated their house help like an unpleasant mess they'd carelessly stepped in, starving them and beating them for every real or imagined infraction.

Lucky looked healthy. Happy even. He scampered away and came back minutes later to mop the floor. And then he went into the kitchen and soon Grace could hear him pounding something. Pestle to mortar. Gari to go with the okra soup. It had been her father's job when she was growing up. He didn't want his wife doing the pounding, he said. Since he couldn't make the soup, the least he could do was make the eba. Not many husbands helped in the kitchen and, up until Ben happened, Grace's mother used to tell Grace to marry a man like her father. After Ben, marriage became something her parents never mentioned again, as if they never expected it to happen. Even without Baby there, she was dented fruit, damaged goods, a bruised tomato. With all the prospective brides men could choose from, why would anyone choose her? Her mother told her this on the day she discovered her daughter's pregnancy. As if marriage was some sort of competition that she had taken herself out of. As if she was a basket of fruit in the market and men were the buyers, pressing her for firmness. Did anyone ask her if, after everything, she even wanted to marry? Did they know just how much Ben had taken from her? And yet, without searching, not really, she had ended up with Okika, a man exactly like her father.

Twenty

Trans-Ekulu, Enugu

2020

Grace's phone was ringing. It was such an odd sound to be invading this space that was tight and coiled like something waiting to spring. It might be Okika, she thought, fumbling in her handbag for it, her heart racing. It was Ifeatu. Grace sighed. She couldn't face taking the call now, but she would have to leave. She tapped out a quick text to her friend. *On my way.* Ifeatu had told her she was coming that day so they could go and meet with a woman who was eager to be put in touch with Grace. The woman had come from Abuja. A very wealthy woman, wife of some government minister. Her identity was to be kept secret until she met with Grace, but the matter the woman wanted to discuss with her was very delicate and involved babies. Grace hoped to be rewarded generously enough to make the whole cloak-and-dagger business worth it.

'This is big fish ooo,' Ifeatu promised her. The woman would only discuss the business face to face because she was worried about her phones being tapped. She did not even want her name mentioned. Grace had forgotten all about it until now. She also could not cancel. Her reputation was built on her being dependable. She had never let anyone down, not once. If she were to start now, it would be the beginning of the tarnishing of her brand. Baby factories were springing up all over. Everyone with a house and a spare bedroom and some knowledge of midwifery felt they could set one up. She knew this because she read of police raiding some of these clinics and 'freeing' young women who looked scared and helpless. Parading them in front of the TV to 'tell their story'. Did these journalists not realize, Grace wondered, that they were doing more harm than good? Exposing the women to public scrutiny destroyed whatever chance they had of living a normal life. Some of the raids happened because the women had been paid less than they had been promised and they tipped off the police out of revenge, willing to go down with the owners as long as the latter were punished. Their greed was their undoing, and Grace had no compassion for them. Once, she watched on TV as one such clinic was bulldozed, crushed to rubble, mere stone and sand as the owner, a man in his sixties with unnaturally white teeth, was forced to watch. The women who had been 'rescued' were sitting on the floor beside the man. Six women in different stages of pregnancy. Grace thought it served him right. He deserved to lose his entire investment. He did not even manage to salvage a pen. You could not take something as precious as a baby from a woman and not compensate her well, Grace said to the TV. She worried about the women. About two of the women looked like teenagers and Grace imagined their fear at that moment. The camera zoomed in on each face as if asking the viewers at home to imprint the faces of the women in their memories. Imagine that, Grace told Okika who was watching the news with her. Imagine that their parents lied to people about where their children were and then they are exposed like this?

'Then they shouldn't have lied,' Okika said. 'I wish our people would stop acting like a girl getting pregnant was the end of the world. If you don't want kids to get pregnant, give them access to sex education.' Okika sounded impatient.

Grace knew that he hated the idea of these clinics, even though she owned one. It was inhumane, he said, but even he could not give Grace an answer when she asked what to do if a pregnant woman of any age came to her and begged her to pay her in exchange for a child they could not keep for whatever reason. 'Do I turn that person away? What would I have achieved?'

'They could always give up the children for adoption, do it the legal way,' he said.

'So either way they give up the children, right? One way – my way – ensures they get adequately compensated. The other way they end up with nothing. So, tell me again, which way is better?'

'I just think that what you do, clinics like yours, unregulated and black-market adoption is worse. You don't know the homes these babies are going to. You don't vet them, you don't offer counselling of any sort to the biological mothers, you just offer them wads of cash and send them out.'

Grace thought Okika sounded out of touch with Nigeria. The years he'd spent in America had him thinking like an oyibo. Did he think that any orphanage in Enugu offered any of those hoity-toity sounding services?

Counselling and follow-up visits and all what-nots, no matter what they claimed to do? They handed babies over, someone made money along the way – not the mothers of the babies – and that was it. 'But we give the mothers money and a chance to lead a normal life,' she said.

'It's always all about money,' Okika said. 'You make money from it too.' His voice was firm. His accusation hurt Grace because it was unfair. It wasn't the money that motivated her. It was the chance to make reparations for her own wrong. And she did know the families the babies were going to. She knew they were families with enough money to look after the babies, because her services did not come cheap. Only the people at the very top could afford her these days. It had been a calculated risk on her part to charge as much as she did, because she wanted to remain exclusive and she wanted whichever unfortunate woman fate sent her way to be recompensed well enough to have a choice to make something of her life. Many of her 'wombs' (and how she hated that word) were poor. The money changed their lives. Okika navigated life as a man, a man with an income that placed him comfortably in the middle class. It was easy for him to live a life where things were either black or white, where life lacked the necessary nuances of the world women inhabited. She let him 'win' the argument.

But some of his fears were coming true, Grace admitted to herself. Some unscrupulous doctors had been arrested for running a 'farm'. These doctors had arranged for over a dozen young women to be abducted. The families thought they had been killed and used for ritual. Kidnappers always asked for ransom, but these doctors kept them hostage in a house in the middle of rural Abakaliki and paid men to rape them and get them pregnant so that the babies could be sold off. One of the women managed to escape. Seven months pregnant and emaciated, both her story and the story of the arrest of the doctors (three women and one man) were headline news for a short while before Boko Haram and herdsmen attacks snatched back the front-page spot. Grace would not be shocked if the doctors had been let go and were back to running their farm again. Money had a loud and intimidating voice in this country. Whoever this woman was, Grace had to meet her. It would be good for her business.

She stood up and told her parents, 'I have to go. I have an appointment I can't miss, but I will be back. As soon as I can. If not today, then tomorrow.' Her legs were shaky as if she hadn't eaten or slept in days. She had to stand still for a while until they steadied before she walked out into the rain, Lucky's slow pounding ringing in her ears.

Twenty-One

Zoo Estate, Enugu

2020

Grace barely paid attention to Ifeatu or the heavily bejewelled woman – a shiny gold ring on each finger – they'd come to see, even though it had stunned her to see who it was. Grace's mind kept drifting back to what she had just learned. Her mother had actually followed her that night, determined to see that her baby came to no harm. She had seen a couple take the infant. She had watched as the couple looked around, probably worried that someone was watching them, and walked off with the baby. Maybe her baby was alive and well, with a family who loved her like the babies that she herself placed with others. Ifeatu was saying something as both women walked behind the potential client. Grace hadn't caught what her friend said, but when Ifeatu said, 'Right, Grace?' Grace had nodded. She should pay attention. The woman – who asked Grace to call her Felly – was one of the country's wealthiest women. It was said that she had made her money even before she met her husband, wealth passed down by her parents who owned a plastic-making business which she and her siblings now ran. Any plastic souvenir given away at any wedding or funeral most likely came from one of their factories. The woman's face was always in the papers, surrounded by her family. She already had children, so what could she be wanting with Grace?

The woman was so light skinned, Grace could see her veins like little worms under her skin when she reached out to shake Grace's hand, even though there was a pandemic and people had been warned to desist from physical contact. In this country, no one did what they were told. And certainly not people as wealthy as Felly. Grace noticed that Felly's knuckles were dark. *Iru Fanta, okpa Coke.* Fanta face, Coca-Cola legs. Grace and her mates used to mock anyone with the tell-tale signs of a complexion that came out of a jar of bleaching cream. No matter how much one bleached, certain body parts defied submission. Felly's skin was so soft, like a baby's. Felly, gold bangles jangling, was walking them through a wide veranda to an ornately furnished sitting room with sculptures everywhere Grace looked.

'We rarely come here, but I was born in Enugu, you know,' the woman said. She locked the door behind them. 'I don't want these servants wandering in here. The walls are soundproof. The deals that have been made here, you wouldn't believe!' She laughed. Grace offered a half laugh. She hadn't seen any domestic staff except the gateman who had let them in, but she imagined that a woman of this stature would not keep a home without help, even if it was one she hardly used. She offered Grace and Ifeatu drinks. Grace was in no mood for a drink, but if there was anything she had learned in her line of work, it was never to refuse the drink of someone wanting to work with you. Especially not one as wealthy as this bulbous woman before her. She accepted a glass of wine, as did Ifeatu. The wine was too sweet for Grace, but she drank it, even complimented it. Ifeatu drained hers too. Felly had a too-loud voice, speaking as if she was used to shouting. Maybe the soundproof room was built for her, Grace thought.

'I have a problem I need you to take care of. You came highly recommended. Highly recommended.' The person who'd introduced her to Ifeatu, who'd introduced her to Grace, was someone she could trust with her life. 'So when she speaks, I listen.' The problem was that her daughter had gone and 'stupidly got herself pregnant. These little girls, they want everything now. Twenty years old, and this is how she wants to throw her life away. I can't let her abort it. I am a Christian, but you understand that she cannot keep the child.'

'What of the boy responsible?' Grace asked.

'Boy? Hm. The idiot has been taken care of. Some nonentity that managed to trick her into bed. The son of a nobody who thought he could get her pregnant and we'd agree to a marriage? God forbid bad thing!' She shuddered. Grace imagined this twenty-year-old, in love with someone her parents considered beneath her station. Had he honestly thought he could twist their hands by planting his baby inside the girl's womb? If he did, then neither he nor Felly's daughter knew how wealthy people in this country operated. It didn't matter what they believed in, how they worshipped; those things did not stand in the way of ensuring that nobody ever forced their hands. 'See the idiot she calls her boyfriend. Spoiled is what she is. Spoiled! Imagine bringing home that rat whose mother sells akara, and his father an ordinary electrician.' She stretched the 'ordinary', spitting it out like something distasteful. 'Imagine her sleeping with him. His grubby hands all over my daughter.' She drained another glass of wine and cracked her knuckles.

'By the time the men I sent after him are done with him, eh. If he sees anyone who looks like my daughter, nobody will tell him to run. A diro agwa ochi nti n'agha e su. No one needs to tell the deaf that a war has broken out.' The woman laughed. Grace flinched. She felt momentary sympathy for the young man who was probably so brutally beaten he ended up with broken bones for falling in love with a woman above his station, but she knew better than to say anything. What was needed from Grace was a private room in her clinic for the daughter. No one was to visit her, no one was to know of her identity. And for Grace to deliver the baby personally, no matter what time of day or night she went into labour. Once the baby was born, Grace was to make sure the daughter did not even hold it.

'Not even for one second. I don't even want to know what sex the baby is. And I don't want her to either.' The woman hissed and said something under her breath, probably cursing her daughter's lover. She addressed Grace again. For her trouble and discretion, Grace would be adequately compensated.

The more the woman spoke, the more Grace regressed in her mind to the day when she herself had been forced to give her baby up. She had at least been allowed to see the baby. What would it do to this girl to not even have that? Grace sighed. She knew what she would like to do, but she also knew what she *would* do, and the two were not the same. She stood up, plastered a smile on her face, extended her hand, and she and Felly shook in agreement. She had survived the loss of her own child; Felly's daughter would survive hers too. That was what it meant to be a woman here: an accumulation of losses starting from childhood. The growing of thick skin. The living with secrets that no one else must know.

Twenty-Two

Between Zoo Estate and Uwani, Enugu

2020

Ifeatu asked Grace what was up as soon as they were out of earshot. 'Nothing,' Grace said, not daring to look at Ifeatu who, in some ways, knew her better than Okika, even though she had not known Grace as long. She regretted agreeing to leave her own car at the clinic so that she and Ifeatu could drive together. Ifeatu would know she was lying and she would not stop until she had a satisfactory answer from Grace. She would never be ready, no matter how much she loved her friend, to share that aspect of her life with her. She had met Ifeatu at an age when she did not think she could still make friends. After the birth of the twins, Grace had started going to the gym, determined to lose the extra weight she had gained in pregnancy, although she had never been thin and Okika said he loved to bury his face in the folds of flesh on her body. Seduced by the TV adverts of a new gym in Achara Lay Out with sleek equipment and testimonials from women looking as if they'd slipped out of the pages of a glamour magazine 'three months postpartum', she had registered on impulse. It was on her first visit that she met Ifeatu.

Ifeatu bore a striking resemblance to Naomi Campbell. She had a sleek, dark complexion and was taller than any woman Grace knew. The two women had shared neighbouring bikes and Ifeatu started a conversation about a film that Grace had incidentally just managed to see that week. 'Have you seen *Missing Angel*? That Dolly is so pretty,' Ifeatu said. She hadn't bothered to introduce herself, speaking as if she'd known Grace for years and she was continuing a conversation that had been interrupted. 'Too fine to play a poor orphan ooo.' Grace laughed and agreed that indeed, Stella who played Dolly looked too fresh to be poor. From *Missing Angel*, they had moved on to other topics, each one initiated by Ifeatu. Grace, raised to be timid, admired people who were not. People who could walk up to strangers at parties and start talking about anything. She had never in her life been the first to initiate a conversation. As a child, even before the secret she could not share, Grace spoke only when spoken to, the way good children were supposed to. Her parents did not encourage her to sit in the sitting room when they had adult guests, or to listen in on adult conversations. When people upset her, she folded into herself rather than confront them. At home, her parents encouraged her quiet studiousness and when she did ask the questions that bothered her, like that time she had asked her mother about sex, she never got answers. So Grace lived in her quietness, but she craved friends, especially when she left primary school and making friends became more difficult. As one of her teachers used to say, 'It is not because one has no appetite that one does not crave food. They are two separate things.'

Grace's secret also meant that for a long time she kept away from people. She had acquaintances in nursing school, but no one ever came close enough to qualify as a friend. Friends put too much of a demand on one that Grace was afraid that her secret would burst out of her and spill out in an unguarded moment. Weeks into their relationship, Okika had taken Grace to meet his friends. A lot that had stunned Grace with their boisterousness. She had thought it was only romantically that opposites were supposed to attract. Their voices drowned Okika's, these three men he'd known since secondary school, and whom he called 'brothers', in a way that meant something because he wasn't close to his own brother who lived in Germany and only came home every four years.

'This your woman is fine ooo, Oki. Do you have any friends as fine as you to introduce me to?' one of them, Emeka, asked, cutting something in Grace. Okika had asked her a few times already if she was hiding him from her family and friends. Her parents were dead but had she no cousins? No one? 'Are you hiding me, babe?' He pulled a mock pained face and held a palm to his heart.

'No,' she said. 'Absolutely not. But I don't have family, I don't have friends. I pretty much come on my own.'

She didn't think Okika believed her, but it was her he was in love with, what did he care about friends and cousins? Even before the secret, she wasn't close to those cousins she saw once every year when they returned to the east for Christmas from Kano and Jos and Lagos, the children of her father's sisters who had married men from other towns and only came back for a day or two to say hello. And, on her mother's side, she saw the three children of her mother's only brother even less. They were much older than her. The year she turned ten, her mother had sent her to Onitsha to vacation with this uncle's family, and that holiday had been the loneliest of her life. Her cousins ignored her and she spent all her days inside the bedroom allocated to her, coming out only to eat. She told her mother, at the end of it, that she never wanted to go back even though her uncle and aunt had given her N200 spending money and she'd felt so rich back then.

Okika assumed she had no friends because she was an introvert, never once suspecting that it was an introversion that she had carefully cultivated. When they planned their wedding and Grace did not have swarms of friends over looking at her wedding dress or helping her choose bridesmaid outfits (and she had none), Okika said he felt sorry for her. Why? She wanted to know. 'Because it feels like a lonely kind of life. Just . . . going through life like this with no one else.'

'But I got you,' she said and kissed him quickly to stop him from seeing the tears gathering in her eyes, threatening to flood down. This was not how she had imagined her wedding to be. Her husband's family and friends and none of hers save the handful of women from nursing school she said hello to. Okika's parents had not hidden the fact that they were disappointed there was no traditional marriage, no carrying of wine to the bride's family.

'It's always important to do things the right way,' Okika's father had told both Grace and Okika. And the right way was taking wine to her people in Osumenyi, where her father's people came from. Even if her father was dead, no Igbo compound was left bereft of a single person to represent dead parents. Grace said she had no one. Her father's compound was empty. For generations, no sons had been born into it. Okika's mother said it was unheard of, a marriage with no one from the bride's family, but they were modern young people and she was old, and what did she know about all the ways in which the world was changing? Grace understood their misgivings; no one trusted a bride or groom with no family. It was a bad sign. When Okika's parents cooled towards her, not speaking to her unless they needed to, she was hurt but she did not blame them. She blamed her own parents. And she blamed Ben, whose deliberate pouring of water over her that afternoon long ago set her life in a direction that had her without a single family member on her wedding day, and ruined the relationship between her and her parents-in-law who sat in a corner, looking like guests rather than the owners of the day.

There had been times, before the wedding, she had feared that they would succeed in discouraging Okika from marrying her, and she told Okika this. He'd laughed in the manner of men who knew that the worst a parent could do with a son they disagreed with was to gently dissuade him, but not lay down the law, telling him what to do as could be so easily done with a daughter. 'I'd have liked to see them try,' he said, and she envied him that certainty.

Ifeatu collected friends like buttons. Early in their friendship, she had invited Grace to nights out with her other friends. Grace went twice: once to a restaurant and once to a club, but she was the only one of the women with two eighteen-month-old twins, and she both tired of and was jealous of the freedom the women had had to be young and *do* things, *see* things. Of the seven friends Grace was introduced to, one was a doctor, one was an engineer, one worked in the same advertising agency as Ifeatu, three were bankers and the last one said she was simply 'a baby girl'. Her parents were wealthy, her boyfriend was wealthy, and she wasn't in a hurry to put her Estate Management degree to use working for anyone. The women were giddy with life and tales of their travels to Dubai and London and Morocco just to hang out because, you know, you only get the one life. No, Grace did not know. She would never know what it was like to be young and not haunted. And if you only lived once, then she'd already squandered that life. She could do worse than Okika. As long as she didn't think too deeply of it, what she felt for him could be described as love, but there were times she wondered if she would have married him and quite so quickly if she hadn't been in a hurry to prove to herself and to her parents that the other life she never spoke of was truly behind her. She was always going to marry the first decent person that asked her to, because despite everything, she was the type of woman who wanted commitment, marriage, family. It was just lucky that it happened to be Okika. Ifeatu's friends intimidated her and made her yearn for things she did not have. Her father used to say that when one starts desiring what one doesn't have, it is greed. 'And greed is the harbinger of all sorts of evil.' She did not know if she agreed with her father, but the women who were close to her in age – but seemed much younger – brought out a discontent in her that had her questioning her marriage for the first time and so she began making excuses not to be out with them. She could take such yearnings in doses, and Ifeatu was dose enough.

Soon, Ifeatu stopped inviting her out with the rest, and

when they met up to hang out, it was just the two of them. She lived her alternative life vicariously through Ifeatu and that greed and envy she'd felt with the rest whittled down to plain admiration, which Grace could deal with. Ifeatu was thirty-six now to Grace's forty-two and marriage wasn't something she was interested in. 'Maybe one day,' she told Grace. 'But Ekene and I are fine as we are, and I love my space, so why ruin it?' Ekene was her boyfriend of several years who she had refused to move in with. Grace used to think she wanted to be a man, but with Ifeatu, she realized that what she wanted was to be allowed the same freedom that men had. Ifeatu had that. And it was what Grace wanted to give her daughters too.

'You're sure nothing is wrong?' Ifeatu said now, taking her eyes off the road for a second to look at Grace. 'I could have sworn your mind was elsewhere all the while we were with Felly. And I've never known you to be almost disinterested in business.'

'Well,' Grace said, and stopped. She started again, careful with her words. 'I am upset she's doing this to her daughter. What if the daughter wants the baby?' Her voice stuck. 'The women I help don't *want* to keep their babies. What if this one does? Her mother is going behind her to . . .' She stopped again. Quickly, before Ifeatu had a chance to say anything, 'And what's wrong with her ending up with a man who isn't wealthy, eh?'

'I know . . . but what's your own? If you don't do it, someone else will, and who knows how that might end up? They are determined to be rid of the baby, and as for the guy, nothing you can do about it. Life sucks, you know.' Grace knew. She had always been as pragmatic as

Ifeatu, but now, her emotions were usurping her rational, practical mind. She ran the clinic. Because she was practical. Women gave away babies and it didn't kill them. It hadn't killed her to have Baby taken from her. None of the arguments she would have used to convince herself worked this time. She couldn't take another woman's baby away from her, especially not if that woman was unwilling, could she? Things that did not kill you did not necessarily leave you fully alive either. They ate you up until you were a carcass of yourself, until no single moment of your life, no matter how joyful, wasn't tinged with loss. For the first time since she'd got into the business, her resolve to be practical faltered.

'You're sure that's all that's on your mind?' Ifeatu asked again. Grace gave her a quick nod.

'You know, the girl and her boyfriend, they will bounce back. They'll be fine.'

Grace said nothing. Suddenly she wanted to get out of the car. She couldn't breathe.

Twenty-Three

New Lay Out, Enugu

2020

Grace drove home rather than return to her parents' house. All through the drive, her insides rattled. The first time she learned the phrase 'tin man', she had imagined that people who were cruel walked around all day, bits of steel clanking around where their heart should be. She wasn't heartless, so why was she feeling this way? The rattling eased the closer she got to her house, and was replaced by a fluttering anxiety in her chest. What if Okika hadn't returned? *Of course he'll have returned. Don't think like that.* She was disappointed not to see Okika's car parked in its usual spot under the shade of the mango tree, rather than in the carport, which was big enough for two cars, but half of which Okika had appropriated for his ping-pong table. Grace had complained at the beginning. What did they need a table for if Okika could play at the club? Grace did not play, but Okika and the twins did, and three out of four meant the table stayed. Grace nosed her car in beside the table. The two bats were still lying on one side of the table, a ball pinned underneath them, same as they were after the twins played before they left on Friday evening. Inside the house, the glass of water with which she had taken her pills was still where she'd left it. Everything seemed the same on the surface. Underneath were the fissures. She had no idea how deep the cracks went or how much damage they'd caused. But Okika loved her. Surely, the cracks were not irreparable.

She had promised her parents she would be back, but now, in the silence of the house, she began to see that what she wanted more than anything else was to be alone, to think without being disturbed. Maybe it was a blessing Okika wasn't home yet after all, she thought. Her head held too much she had to offload and process without any distraction. The meeting with Felly, what she was being asked to be a part of, had left her unsettled. Rehoming a baby with the mother's consent and paying the mother was completely different from colluding with a mother to have her grandchild taken away at birth without the mother's knowledge, let alone consent. Felly's instructions were clear. Find a new parent for the baby and make sure the daughter did not spend any time at all with the infant. The same thing that had happened to Grace. This was a line she shouldn't cross. She couldn't let history repeat itself.

The house smelled strongly of the disinfectant they'd asked Cee to start using once the pandemic started. At the beginning, she had kept the twins home even though their very expensive private school assured them it was safe for kids to come. The rain had stopped, but through the open windows Grace could smell the wet earth rising above the smell of the disinfectant. She closed all the blinds and sank into a chair, replaying the events of the day, from the revelation that her mother had trailed her and Baby that night, to Felly's daughter who would be arriving in a week's time, even though she was only four months gone, believing that she was only coming to Enugu to get the best care and keep away from prying eyes. The daughter of a minister, it would be difficult to keep her delivery a secret once she had the baby. 'Foolish girl,' Felly had said. 'She thinks she can have the bastard in our house?' Grace did not often get involved in the lives of her patients or her clients. She'd always managed to keep everything professional, but this one bothered her. The amount Felly was throwing at her was enough to expand her clinic, and have some left over to invest in some sort of empowerment programme for young girls from poor homes. Maybe computer programming workshops for those interested. And something for widows. She had dreamed of this too. Setting up training programmes for poor, uneducated widows so that they gained billable skills. Or maybe she could set up a scheme where poor single women would be given seed money to set up some petty business.

For once, she wouldn't be paying the new mother. Neither Felly nor her daughter needed her money. And she was being paid handsomely too. People like the minister and his wife literally had the country's wealth for their personal use, so why should she, Grace, feel bad about benefitting from it? She would simply be getting her just share of the national cake. The more she thought about it, the more convinced she was that she would be doing more good than harm, and so the better she felt. Finally, she pushed whatever nagging guilt she might have been feeling about what she would be complicit in – lying to the girl that she would return to Lagos with her baby – and turned her thoughts to Okika.

Surely, he had sulked long enough. When he came back, they'd have to have a long talk. If he wanted her parents in their lives, she would let him. Now she thought of it, she remembered that, not long ago, the girls had gone through a phase of wanting grandparents. More than wanting, they had craved it. They would be thrilled – if confused – that they were not grandparent-less as they had thought after first Okika's father died when they were ten and his mother eight months later of a broken heart. The girls had been devastated; they had adored their grandmother, who used to come and visit with bags full of icheku, their skins black and velvety. Grace taught the girls to peel the orange flesh from the seed and soak the flesh in water to make 'Fanta' like she had as a child. Cee would vacuum after the girls, picking up bits of the cracked skin littering the floor like ants. As a child, her parents had scolded her for making 'Fanta' from the fruit even though all the other children she knew did it. They never gave her a satisfactory answer as to why she couldn't. And so she only did it when they were out. It wasn't even sweet, the solution of icheku in water, but to kids who hardly ever got soda, unless there was a party or at Christmas, it was a treat to pretend to be drinking the real thing. Grace's twins only drank soda occasionally, but it was by choice. They were watching their weight, talking about calories and genes that predisposed them to gain weight. They were beautiful, Grace told them, and it didn't matter what they weighed. 'You don't get it, Mom!' one of the girls yelled at her. Grace wasn't sure what she didn't get. That they were beautiful or that they didn't need to count calories. She wished they would just enjoy being young and having everything they could ever dream of. They read *Vogue* and *Cosmopolitan* and followed models on Instagram and pinched their sides to show her that they did need to watch their weight and loudly scolded her to 'Stop already, Mom. You don't get it!'

She wanted them to be loud and joyful and confident. When they were born, she read all the books she could find on raising confident kids and practiced each one. She praised them when they did well, never yelled at them and answered every question they asked her, no matter how uncomfortable. She was intentional about it and asked Okika to be the same.

When the twins returned, if their father wasn't home then, they'd want to know why. And Grace – who had sworn never to lie to her children, never to evade their questions – would have to tell them that she had been living a lie their entire lives. Grace needed a drink. Something stiff. She poured herself a whiskey and, once again, she wished that she still smoked. She'd given up once she started trying to get pregnant with Okika, expecting it to happen as quickly as it had the first time, when she hadn't been trying at all, hadn't even known what she was doing. She had never understood it, how difficult it had been to get pregnant again once she was ready. It had seemed to her that her body was taunting her. And once she had become pregnant with the girls, she was stunned that her body acted as if this was her first pregnancy, as if it had forgotten that she had done it before. The morning sickness was worse than it had been with Baby. Nothing about the pregnancy with the twins had felt familiar at all.

A cigarette would have calmed the storm raging in her. It would have calmed the panic rising in her, as hours passed, and she began to imagine that the unthinkable might happen, that Okika might not come back and she'd have no choice but to face the girls alone before she was ready. She walked to the open window and shouted for the guard. 'Arinze, come here. Go buy me cigarette.'

Grace did not return to her parents' house. Not that day or in the days after. She found that she was better able to think away from them. Better able to maintain her anger at them, at Ben, at Ben's parents, at the woman who wanted her daughter's baby taken from her, at the world. In the isolation of her own house, a home she lived in with the family that she'd made herself, a home she'd filled with memories that did not include her past, she could again dredge up the righteous anger she had harboured all those years. It was fuel for her success. Here, she could feel rage again at her mother for turning up the way she had with no thought as to how she could ruin her daughter's life. And for what? To ask her to forgive the people she had no intention of ever forgiving, people that, had they ever turned up before Grace, she would have done everything in her power to crush them the way they had crushed her. So what if Ben was dead? What he had done to her was worse than death. She didn't care. All she cared about was that her husband returned. So she stayed home and waited for Okika. She called his number every few minutes, listening each time as it rang out and then started going straight to voicemail, an automated voice announcing, 'The MTN subscriber you're calling is not available right now. Please leave a message after the beep.' Grace understood that he'd switched his phone off, and none of his friends admitted to having seen him. Instead she used her phone to play music by Flavour and Phyno and Olamide and Wizkid to numb the sadness. She left the TV on like she did when she stayed at hotels to pretend someone was present, having a conversation with her. She toyed with the idea of driving down to Mgbwo, even though she knew it was unlikely that Okika would have gone to a house that he hadn't been to since his mother died. And if for some reason he did want to visit, it would not be in the middle of a pandemic. He'd want to be somewhere he had easy access to water and hand sanitizer and take-out food. Is it his uncles' wives that would be running around getting him food and water and all? Besides, the last time Okika was there to prepare the family home for his father's funeral, Grace had to send the driver down with coolers of food from Enugu because the kitchen Okika had once furnished, with a six-burner gas cooker and a dining table big enough to sit four, had been stripped of everything. The cupboards were empty of the chinaware Okika had gifted his mother over the years. The forks and knives and spoons with ornamental heads his mother had liked were all gone. Someone – probably his uncles and their wives – had gone to work before Okika arrived. He could not mention the looting without being accused of being disrespectful, and so he ate the food Grace sent through the driver, ate off the plates it came on, used the cutlery Grace sent and delivered everything back with the driver once he was done. Also, Grace knew that he wouldn't want to be anywhere that the uncles had easy access to him. He had no interest in 'being a good son', as they constantly badgered him to be by knocking down his father's bungalow and putting up a more lavish duplex or even a three-story building. 'You can afford to,' his youngest uncle told him when the uncle visited a while ago, reeling off the names of how so and so's son, whose house in Enugu wasn't even as huge as Okika's, had built a house that looked like a 'London cathedral', and people came from everywhere to gawk at it. Okika joked once to Grace that he was sure the uncles wanted him to build the house in Mgbwo so that they could move in; they were already using his father's house. One had set up a chicken coop in the backyard and he'd heard rumours that the youngest uncle rented out rooms in the house. Okika didn't care and neither did Grace. They were born in Enugu, their children were born in Enugu, Enugu was home. Why spend money building a house in a place they never even visited anymore? Grace did not get it. All over Igbo towns, people built palatial homes they'd never live in but the roads to the houses were rutted and dusty. Some of the communities had no electricity. Just these empty mansions sticking out of a dark and dusty earth like shiny toys abandoned in the middle of a desert. It was like looking at a wound. At least she and Okika agreed on that: they would not be contributing to any such nonsense.

Sunday morning came, and Grace was sure that Okika would return. She got out of bed and began to tidy a house that did not need tidying. She wiped down the pictures on the mantelpiece, dusted the arms of the sofa, sheathed in crocheted covers like sofas were in Grace's youth. The kitchen was spotless, but Grace scoured and cleaned and sweated. She brewed coffee, made toast and set the table. When she heard footsteps, she jumped up. The twins walked in, their face masks under their chins, the way Grace often scolded them about. Grace had not been expecting them home so soon. And Okika was still unreachable. 'Wear those masks properly or not at all,' she snapped at her daughters before they'd even had a chance to say hello to her. She pretended not to see the girls look at each other, pretended not to hear the 'What's biting her?' that Kaikele muttered under her breath at Mmuodum as they walked by her and disappeared down the corridor into their rooms.

Twenty-Four

New Lay Out, Enugu

2020

All of Sunday passed and Okika did not come back. Grace did not move from the sitting room; she had wanted to see Okika before the girls did. They had to decide together how much the girls needed to know, and if they told the girls about Grace's parents being alive, they had to decide together how best to tell them. Grace would prefer not to tell them at all, but the genie was out of the bottle. There was no putting it back in. If her daughters saw they had a united front, she and Okika, they'd be more likely to understand her motives for pretending for years that her parents were dead. No matter how many times she imagined she heard the gate creak open and Okika's car drive in, sending her to the window to confirm; no matter how often she imagined she heard his voice, raising a scintilla of hope in her chest, he did not return. This was what it was like when someone died, Grace thought. When her paternal grandmother died, her father swore that he saw her around the house, that he heard her in the shower. It had scared the young Grace to hear her father because she worried about bumping into this ghost that left the dead to haunt the son she'd left behind. Now, she knew there had been no ghost, it was simply her father's grief taking shape and conjuring images of his mother and her voice to him. But Okika was not dead. He had simply gone away. Maybe that was a sort of death, Grace thought. He was, after all, unreachable. Fortunately, the girls, wrapped up in their teenage selves, had not yet asked of him. They hadn't even left their rooms, from where Grace could hear heavy metal (Mmuodum's) and an occasional giggling on the phone (Kaikele's). It wasn't until dinnertime, when Grace sat stony faced through the pasta that Mmuodum thawed and heated up, that the twins appeared to notice that their father hadn't been home the whole day.

'Where's Dad?' Mmuodum asked, twirling pasta around her fork, barely looking up from her food.

'Out.' Grace took a forkful of food, not even tasting it. For all she knew, she might have been chewing cardboard. She asked Kaikele, who was closest to her, to please pass her the cheese.

'When's he back?' Mmuodum asked again.

Grace did not know. There must have been something in her tone because Mmuodum stole a glance at Kaikele sitting beside her and no word was exchanged again. Not about their father missing at the table, not about Grace's clear irritability. Forks and knives clanged; the AC hummed a steady, low sound. Grace and Okika had made it a family tradition, ever since the girls were young, always to eat Sunday dinner together. All the other days, everyone was free to do what they wanted and eat whenever they desired, but Sunday dinner was sacrosanct. It was the way Sunday Mass had been for Grace in her childhood, a family affair. It had given their Sundays a sense of ceremony which delighted Grace. Her husband and her two girls surrounding her, eating together, at the same time every Sunday. Rituals were important, she told her children when they complained. This time last week, there had been nothing to suggest that today would be different. What had they eaten? Rice and fish stew, peppered tilapia. Cee's specialty. Mmuodum, the more talkative of her girls, had them laughing through dinner, recounting the story of a classmate whose father had wandered into view during their Zoom class, clad only in his boxers, cleaning out his ear with a finger, his stomach wobbling like jelly. 'It was so disgusting,' Mmuodum said. 'Our Chemistry teacher was so embarrassed; she literally couldn't stop sputtering the rest of the lesson.'

'I'd die if I were his child,' Kaikele said.

'Parents live to embarrass their children, don't you know?' Okika said, to which Mmuodum swore that if he ever did that to her, she'd *literally* move out of the house, move out of the city, move out of the country even. 'How could I face anyone after that?'

'No one is moving out anywhere,' Grace said. She was certain that this world she had meticulously created would always be there, unchanged. At least until the girls began university. For now, they'd always have Sunday dinners together, eating whatever meal Cee left in the freezer for them, keeping this ritual of theirs alive. If Okika was missing dinner, then he didn't intend to come back today. He knew that the girls would notice; his staying away was deliberate. He wanted the girls to know that something was wrong and he wanted Grace to deal with it.

Grace breathed in. It was as if her nostrils were clogged. Her head was splitting. She pushed her plate away, pushed her chair back and stood up. 'Listen,' she said. 'Your father hasn't been home since Friday.' She heard, rather than saw the twins drop their forks at the exact same time.

'What's wrong? Did something happen to Dad?' Mmuodum's voice rose in panic.

Grace shook her head and dropped into the chair again. Against her will and to her children's alarm, Grace shut her eyes and began to cry. A loud snorting she didn't know she had in her took over her. Mmuodum (or was it Kaikele?) stood behind her and began to rub her back the way Grace had done to the girls when they were younger. Nothing had happened to their father, she said. She opened her eyes. Kaikele was still sitting beside her, a worried look on her face. Mmuodum stopped rubbing her back and stood behind her sister's chair. Grace wiped her eyes and tried to get herself under control. She had to tell the girls. She had to tell them everything. Tell them she had no idea where their father was, that she hadn't been able to reach him, that she didn't know when he would be back. Tell them about her mother coming to the house. When she opened her mouth, the words would not come, so she said instead, 'We had a disagreement . . . Nothing serious. He'll be back. He's staying at Uncle Efe's.'

It was only a half lie; she could live with that.

Twenty-Five

New Lay Out, Enugu

2020

Grace could not sleep that night. She tossed and turned and, by the time dawn cracked, she felt like she hadn't slept at all. But if she stayed in bed, her daughters would know that something was gravely wrong. Grace never slept in. She could not deal with the questions that would be sure to follow. So she got up once she heard Cee come in and began to get ready for breakfast and work. Somewhere, in the recesses of her mind, she was convinced that if she lived like this was an ordinary Monday, it would turn out to be an ordinary Monday. Outside, Grace could hear the world already stirring. Someone's dog barked. Another responded. A cacophony of car horns slashed the air. Why could these drivers not drive without honking as if they were in a competition with each other? She had thought at some point over the years that it might be a good idea to move to a quieter part of town, maybe to some secluded neighbourhood of the Zoo Estate where one could spend an entire day without hearing a car horn, but living in New Lay Out had its benefits. She had easy access to her clinic, to markets, to church, to the beating heart of Enugu. Nights when she was unable to sleep, she could stand on her balcony and just watch life happening. From her kitchen, she heard the world. If she moved to somewhere more exclusive, she would miss that. A car with an exhaust pipe letting out a sound like a bad subwoofer of a stereo drove by. A new itinerant preacher was ringing the ubiquitous bell all preachers carried, and preaching about the end of the world and illuminati. *Pray! Pray for the end is near. The globalists want to end the world, but our God is a mighty one.* Grace wondered if the man knew what or who exactly *the globalists* were. Or even the illuminati. And did this person even have a mask on? The preacher was now talking of George Floyd. *Pray for our brother, Floyd. Pray that his soul rests or else . . .*

Grace did not hear the rest, for the preacher's words were swallowed by a breakfast hawker. *Buy tea. Buy bread. Buy tea. Buy bread.* It was only when Grace watched foreign news or heard the NCDC ads on the radio, reminding people about social distancing, to wear masks, wash their hands, that Grace remembered that there was a global pandemic. In Enugu, apart from the concession to mask-wearing by some, life moved on almost as normal.

Grace allowed her thoughts to drift to all the work she had ahead of her today. The couple coming in at ten. A smile crept onto her face, already anticipating their delight, their gratitude. This was what she was created to do. Nothing else. This was the only way she could make up for that night when she could not stand up to Ben, his mother and to her own parents. What was ripped out of her that night could never be replaced, but the hollowing of her that followed could be patched up in bits. In life, she had learned, one patched up as best as one could because sometimes that was all that one could do. Yet, this morning, as she stood by the corridor to Mmuodum and Kaikele's rooms, Okika gone, the force of her loss hit her as if it was new. Grace took in a long, deep breath and pushed open Mmuodum's door. The twins were in the same bed, identical even in sleep. She planted a soft kiss on each forehead. They smelled of the lavender body and hair shampoo they had recently become so fond of that Grace imported the bottles in cartons from the US. There was nothing her children wanted that she could not get them and the power this gave her stunned her even now. She, Grace, whose future her mother had said was ruined. *You've wasted your life. Whatever will become of you now?* 'Well, Mother,' she said. 'This is what has become of me. I am rescuing other children.' She was now one of the most respected women in Enugu. Soon her driver would report for work, the gateman would swing the gates open and her day would begin. Same as always. If Okika never came back? She still had her twins. She told Cee that no, there was no need to make anything for Oga; he'd travelled. She asked Cee to check in on the girls in an hour to make sure they were up and getting ready to log in to school by eight-thirty, and then Grace, as she did every weekday, walked out to her car.

The sight of her driver, Odiuko, dressed in his blue uniform and shiny black shoes, standing by the car ready for her as always, soothed her. She responded to his 'Good morning, ma' with a smile wider than she would normally give him on a Monday morning, preoccupied with all the things she had to do in the week ahead. The drive to Uwani on Monday mornings often took close to forty minutes, with Zik Avenue unpassable unless there was a police warden on duty. But today, the drive took less than twenty minutes.

It was as if the universe aligned to make her morning as stress free as possible because, when she got into her clinic, it was to walk into the news that the twenty-year-old Emilia who had been with them for three months had gone into labour and Grace had arrived in time to deliver the baby if she wanted to. And she did. She still liked to deliver the babies, to be the one to hold the babies first, to smell them, to hear them send out their first cries into the world. But she particularly wanted to deliver Emilia's. Emilia had come to her emaciated and looking lost. Her parents had thrown her out once they discovered she was pregnant, but her boyfriend, a thirty-five-year-old welder, had taken her in. It did not mollify her parents because the man did not come from the same state as Emilia's family and was not someone they approved of. 'And a mechanic? My parents thought that I'd bring them back a doctor or a lawyer. But from where? Did they train me and send me to school where I'd meet a doctor or lawyer? Do they come to hairdressing schools to look for wives?' Emilia was the only girl of four, and while her struggling parents invested in sending her brothers to school, Emilia was asked to look for a trade – after all, a man would marry her and look after her. She was beautiful enough to attract the right sort of man, so why had she given all that up for an 'ordinary mechanic'? They wouldn't even meet the man who'd wanted to marry her. He had welcomed Emilia into his one-bedroom flat, but it had become too much. During lockdown, they quarrelled a lot. Stuck in a flat Emilia said was the size of an Indomie carton, they got on each other's nerves. The day he told

Emilia that he was doing her a favour, taking her in, looking after her, she decided to come to the clinic where she'd heard that if she was ready to give her baby up, she would get free prenatal care, free lodging and enough money to stand on her feet once the baby was born and taken from her. 'Is it true, ma?' she had asked Grace that day. Her hair was cut short in a secondary-school-girl's fashion. Instead of a mask, she had a head-scarf tied over her face, its tail tucked into the hem of her T-shirt. Her eyes were red as if she had been crying.

'Do you want to give up your child? It's not an easy thing to do, you know.'

Emilia's eyes had shifted from Grace's face to the table between the two, and then to her own hands and the bracelet she was fiddling with on her left wrist. 'It's not what I want, ma. I have no money, no man, no job. I cannot keep the baby. What will I feed it? Where would we live? People like me have no choice.' Her voice, brittle like dry grass rising and falling, and swallowed by the room, broke something in Grace. She wished she could give this girl enough money to set her up and still have her keep her baby, but she was practical enough to know that even with the finances to raise the child, being a twenty-year-old single mother in Enugu was not a choice anyone with common sense would make. Grace made sure Emilia got everything she wanted. Whatever she craved to eat – goat head, abacha, ice cream – the nurses were ordered to give her. Grace stopped by Emilia's room often. Unlike the other patients, she encouraged Emilia to talk to her, to tell her about her fears and her desires. She calmed the fears and swore to Emilia that, one day, she would be able to go to university and get the accounting degree she wanted.

Emilia's eyes lit up when Grace, scrubbed and dressed, walked into the labour room. Grace checked her dilation and asked that she be moved immediately to the delivery room.

'The baby wanted to wait for you,' Emilia said between puffs. She had refused an epidural, which did not surprise Grace. Many of the women she saw wanted to go through the pain of labour and delivery, some sort of mortification for what they had done or were about to do. Grace had given up trying to convince them. Everyone coped in their own way.

Twenty-Six

New Lay Out, Enugu

2020

It was two weeks before Okika got in touch and, when he did, it wasn't with Grace but with their daughters. The twins had stopped asking Grace where their father was and Grace had given up calling his phone every second, hoping that this time he would pick up. She had stopped calling his friends to ask if any of them knew where he was, and when they said no, torturing herself with what they knew and what they were hiding from her. If he wasn't going to do the right thing, she could not force him. He had to return when it suited him, and then they could have the conversation that she had been saving. He could not avoid her and the children forever. She had not been back to see her parents either, and there were days she thought that they didn't even exist, that she hadn't been to their home in Trans-Ekulu, hadn't held her father like a bird in her arms, hadn't felt the tug of something that might be love for the two people she had spent a long time despising. It was a good thing her mother had not come back to the house to look for her; she would have thrown her out. So what if her mother had followed her out that night? What was that against the greater injustice of letting her throw away her own child like a piece of garbage? And how was she even sure her mother was telling her the truth? About trailing her, about seeing a nice young couple pick up the child? How convenient. If she, Grace, had lied for years, why would her own mother not make up lies to make it easier for her to sleep at night? If her mother cared that much, why would she ask her to forgive the people responsible for the worst thing that had ever happened to her? Grace had blocked the image of her mother crying, of her father hugging her, of the smell of home she'd once known. Instead, she had thrown herself into her job, although her legs felt more and more like lead each time she walked into the clinic, and when she slept at night, she did not have a peaceful rest. She no longer just saw her baby's face in her dreams, but the faces of the other babies she had placed. She had stopped trying to figure out what it meant, if it meant anything at all. Cee had stopped setting a place at the table for Okika and didn't ask if she should, although Grace saw the question in Cee's eyes. They might treat her well, but Grace was glad to see that Cee knew her place as a help. She would have hated to have sacked her for insolence. The house had settled into its new existence, shrinking and expanding in all the places Okika's absence had made it necessary for it to. Then, on a Sunday afternoon, Okika had texted the twins to ask if they wanted to 'hang out with me, we have things to discuss.' He'd rather not come to the house, he'd rather they came alone, and he'd send a car for them. Mmuodum showed their mother the text and Grace thought there was something desperate in the words 'hang out'. Whatever

Okika wanted to discuss with them, he wanted to come out of it untainted by whatever Grace might have told them. She knew then that Okika was not coming back. He had made a break and he wanted to make it clear to Grace, otherwise why would he have sent that text? He knew she would see it and he did not care.

When Grace was young, before things changed, she'd overheard her mother and her friends talking about a woman whose husband left her. He'd just walked out of the house one morning as if he was going to work but he did not come back for dinner. Instead, he'd sent a small child, someone's maid, to tell the wife that he was gone. He didn't even have the courage to face the woman himself, Grace remembered her mother saying, and one of the women with her mother had said something along the lines of how men never had courage. 'They just strut along like they do.' Grace wondered if it was courage that Okika lacked. She wasn't sure. What she herself felt was something like hurt, but, after the girls left and she scratched at it, she understood that what she felt was disappointment. After all these years with Okika, he could not even face her. If that was how he wanted it, Grace would not beg. Her mother had not come back to her house either. It was as if, having lit the fire, she had disappeared again to allow Grace douse it however she could. Well, Grace thought, she could do without any of them.

If Okika never came back, if this became any more permanent, she would have to tell her best friend. And then she would have to tell her about Baby. And her parents. It occurred to her that she felt worse about lying to Ifeatu than she did about lying to Okika. Marrying him had been a practical choice. Now, she wondered if that was enough, because when she thought of losing him, she thought of the inconvenience of it. Having to tell people they had broken up, worrying if he would tell the world her biggest, darkest secret. She knew that if she told Ifeatu, her friend would never tell another soul. But Okika? She didn't really know him that well, after all.

Twenty-Seven

New Lay Out, Enugu

2020

From the day her twins were born, Grace's biggest fear was to lose them. They had almost slipped away in the womb, dissolving into clots of blood into the toilet bowl as had happened with a previous pregnancy. She had just gone past the first trimester when she began to feel the familiar pangs of period pain. She believed she was being punished for having got rid of her first, that she would never be forgiven even though she had been too young to have any say in the matter. Did karma really care that she hadn't been mature enough to stand up to her parents? For days after, she would not eat anything, and kept telling Okika that it was her fault. Not understanding why she would think so, Okika consoled her, told her, 'Of course it's not,' and fed her bits of toast soaked in milk as if she were a tiny animal that he'd rescued and was trying to keep alive.

If she lost the twins, two little beings she had already seen on the ultrasound, their little hearts beating so strongly that the doctor had congratulated her, as if she had anything to do with it, if she lost the babies she had already started shopping for, she did not think that she would survive it. She told Okika this and he told her not to be silly, she would not lose them. And if she did, they'd just try again. Grace hated how flippant he sounded. Did he think it was easy to lose pregnancy after pregnancy? She threw the words at Okika who just kept saying calmly, 'They are my babies too. You did not get yourself pregnant. Do you think I'm not hurting also?' She said no, she did not think so, and felt some satisfaction in seeing a look of pain settle on Okika's placid face. That was the first time she wondered if she would have ended up with a man like Okika had she had a normal childhood. He reminded her of water in a bucket. Nothing stirred him. If she lost the twins, she swore to herself, she would leave him. She would live by herself, forswear marriage. Who cared what anyone thought of a woman her age still single? What was she scared of?

In the end, Okika was right. Mmuodum and Kaikele were tenacious. After the panic they caused in their fourth month, they had hung on until they were fully formed and had slipped out into the world holding hands and wearing identical frowns on their wrinkled new baby faces as if they could not believe that they were coming out to *this*. A bright light in a white room gleaming from cleanliness, so sanitized that it seemed lifeless; a doctor, two nurses and their father in surgical caps and gowns and their mother, hair in disarray, lying in bed, legs splayed, panting still from the effort of their passage. They did not look impressed. Whatever they had imagined life outside of the womb to be, it was not this sterile room with nothing to hold their attention. Grace loved them on sight, she did, but her first thought, which remained unvoiced, was that they did not look as beautiful as the one she could not keep. This thought obliterated the radiance of the joy she had expected to feel.

She knew it was silly to think like that, especially after all the effort she had gone through to forget, but she thought it all the same. It trotted into her mind uninvited. When Okika held the babies up, one in each crook of his arm, and said, as if he could read her mind, 'Aren't these the loveliest babies ever?' she had nodded, but her mind was on Baby. She'd thought that once she had other children, she'd cease to think of her firstborn. She would have to learn to hold a place in her heart for Baby and love her new twins. Deep inside her, she harboured a secret fear that they too would leave her.

When her mother-in-law came to stay for a few months and perform omugwo, Grace being motherless, she had not ceded the care of the infants to their grandmother. Grace insisted on bathing the girls herself. She fed them for as long as possible. Their warmth against her chest comforted her. It assured her of the solidity of their presence. She did not hand them over to the grandmother waiting to burp them like she was supposed to after each feed. Instead, Grace burped them herself. Okika's mother complained loudly and bitterly about this new mother who would not let her do what she had come to Enugu to do. 'I didn't leave Mgbwo to come here and sightsee. There's enough to do and see in Mgbwo. I left my farm to come and do right by you since you have no mother to do these things for you.' She did not just sound annoyed, Grace thought. She sounded accusing, as if she was blaming Grace for not having a mother. If Grace had not somehow lost her mother, she would not be here in the city, her farm in the hands of hired hands she could not supervise, her husband's meals prepared by an unsupervised niece who could not be trusted to pick all the stones out of rice. Good manners prevented Grace from telling her she wasn't wanted, that she could go home, go back to her husband and her farm. Grace could do it all by herself and she wanted to. She did not want the children out of her sight. But Grace still did not surrender the babies despite the complaints and the quiet cajoling of Okika, to whom his mother complained incessantly. She could not understand such disrespect, such ingratitude, the older woman said. And such obsession with new babies.

'You know she watches them when they sleep? She just stands there.' She pointed in the general direction of the two matching cots in a corner of the sitting room where the girls slept during the day. 'She just stands there and watches them. You should do something. Talk to her. Her head is not correct.'

Okika talked to Grace. Asked her to allow his mother to bathe the twins. To allow her to carry them when they cried. Grace said okay, but nothing changed. After nine weeks, Okika's mother left, the relationship with her daughter-in-law as frosty as it was when Grace had first said she had no family, so there was no need for a traditional marriage. She did not fight Okika when he suggested they drove to Mgbwo to visit his parents. And she did not fight him when he took the girls to spend weekends with them because his mother wanted to see them. When Okika's mother visited, Grace did not interfere when she spent time with Mmuodum and Kaikele, braiding their hair, colonizing the kitchen so that she could make their favourite meals. She did not intervene when Okika's mother kept the girls up late so they could listen to her folktales. Grace no longer watched them sleep, but the fear was still there. This fear was a formless sort. When she thought of losing the girls, she did not imagine them mangled in a car crash, their blood soaking the floor underneath their seats. Or the girls drowning and floating at the bottom of a pool like children playing angels in the sand. Or dying in a housefire. She did not imagine any such gruesome fate. She did not even imagine a death. They simply vanished. Smoke, spiralling into the air and dissipating. There would be nothing to hold on to. No body. No corpse to cry over. And now, she feared that she could lose them in a different way. They could choose to never come home again, and what would that do to her?

Twenty-Eight

New Lay Out, Enugu

2020

The twins came back from visiting their father on Sunday evening, dragging mud and a cold draft into the house. Grace was relieved to have them back. She tried to hug Mmuodum. The girl held her hands out in front of her to break the hug. There was a new restlessness to Kaikele, who lingered by the front door as if debating whether to come in or not. 'Come in and shut the door,' Grace said to her. 'You're letting mosquitoes in.'

'We want to live with Daddy,' Mmuodum blurted out. And then ran to her room.

Grace looked at her disappearing back, then looked at Kaikele who would not meet her eyes. She said, 'You can't, I forbid it.' Her words carried no conviction. She knew if they wanted to go, and Okika wanted them to, there was nothing she could do. They would not have brought it up if they had not discussed it with Okika. Maybe it was even Okika who had asked them to move in with him, wherever he was. She began to say something to Kaikele, but she too darted past her, down the corridor into their part of the house. She did not ask them what their father had told them. She could tell from the coldness in their eyes, in their voices when they spoke to her, in how Mmuodum had pushed her away and Kaikele whizzed past her, an olivaceous blur in her favourite dress. Still, Grace went after the girls, shouting, 'Your father shouldn't have . . .' But her voice was drowned by the sound of too-loud music, too-loud laughter (or was it cries?) coming from one of their rooms.

The girls had always been close, a fact that Grace had loved and encouraged. Now, they were bonded together in their twinness against their mother. Grace fumbled in her bag unsuccessfully for a cigarette. She couldn't find one. Her hands shook. If she lost the girls too, she did not know how she would cope. She banged on Kaikele's door from which she could hear both their voices. 'Please, let me in,' she screamed. They could not hear her, not above the racket they were making, but Grace kept banging and pleading until she collapsed in a heap outside the door. She needed to smoke, but her frantic rooting through her bag had yielded no result. She covered her face with hands and began to cry, bawling and dripping snot into her palms. She would stay there until the girls came out and told her they were sorry.

Grace didn't know when she fell asleep, but when she woke up, still outside Kaikele's door, her muscles cramping, it was to a quiet house, except for the TV still on in the living room. She wondered what time it was. The girls hadn't come out to apologize. She raised herself, went to the sitting room to turn off the TV and then dragged herself to bed. Now, with the house as quiet as it was, she had calmed down and could think properly. There was no way the girls would leave her to stay with their father, no matter what Okika had told them. Tomorrow, she promised herself, she would tell them her own side of the story. She would tell them everything, tell them she was sorry she hadn't told them sooner, and ask them to imagine how it was for her, young and with a baby she could not keep. She would make them understand why she'd had to keep it a secret. She and the twins were close; they could not abandon her like Okika had. She fell back into an easy sleep. But when she woke up and went to the girls' bedrooms to kiss them good morning, neither girl was in her room.

It was Cee who told her that, as she was arriving for work, Oga Okika was driving out with Mmuodum and Kaikele. 'Is everything okay, ma?' Cee asked, hesitant, her voice low in its deference. Grace nodded quickly, too quickly. Without having breakfast, she left as soon as her driver arrived.

All day at work, Grace could not concentrate, and when she returned in the evening, she did not eat any of the food Cee placed before her. It felt to her as if she had come down with something. Her tongue was bitter. Her body weighed heavily on her. She wondered if it was COVID. She had received a negative result the last time she checked – she and her employees got tested every week – and her sense of smell and taste had not gone. She went to bed and the next day, when she did not come out of bed for breakfast, Cee timidly walked in with a tray of toast and a jug of coffee. 'Madam, you have to eat,' Cee said. She left the tray on the bedside table and walked out. Grace turned her face away from the food and, although she could not sleep, she shut her eyes.

She stayed in bed like that until Ifeatu walked in and drew the curtains. 'What's going on?' her friend asked. 'Cee called me, told me you needed a friend.' Grace started crying and then, before she could change her mind, she told Ifeatu everything. She needed to offload. And once she started, she held nothing back. How could she have thought that she could keep this from her best friend? When she finished, Ifeatu held her like a child and fed her the toast, which had gone cold and hard but she did not mind; it wasn't like she could stomach anything. And then Ifeatu asked her to take a shower. 'I'll leave but I'll come back tonight and stay with you. And tomorrow, even if I have to drag you, you're going into work.'

Twenty-Nine

New Lay Out, Enugu

2020

Grace tried to live as if her mother hadn't turned up, as if her husband and children hadn't left her on her own. She was being treated like a pariah by her own family. The one thing her parents had tried to save her from, and she had tried to avoid, had found her in her own home. Everything she had worked for – husband and children – were gone and the only thing she had left was the clinic. Even though there was a pandemic, or perhaps *because* there was a pandemic, she had more 'buying' customers than she had pregnant women. She had heard of someone with a clinic like hers in Port Harcourt who paid vulnerable young women to get pregnant and give up the babies to keep their supplies up. With things as difficult as they were, there were always willing women to be found, but Grace could not do that. That was like keeping slaves to breed labourers on a plantation, or animals to breed for food, and Grace did not know how anyone with any sort of conscience could justify it. Even if she were to close down her business today, she thought to herself, she had enough saved up to live comfortably for a while – but why should she? She enjoyed what she did. It gave her a sense of purpose, which was why she had not noticed discontent begin to creep up on her, an ant unobserved until the day she drove into her office and she no longer felt the satisfaction that permeated every pore in her body. Maybe it started when she thought that she should turn Felly down. She just needed to find the right time, gather enough courage, be sure it was what she really wanted to do.

Maybe it started the day Emilia's baby was born, and Grace felt the strong desire to foist the baby on the girl. 'Take your baby and go before you regret it,' she wanted to say, even though she knew it would be a foolish thing to do. Emilia's baby came out slippery and slight. A beautiful thing with her mother's squished nose. Emilia turned her head to the side as if the baby were a too-bright object she could not bear to look directly at. This should have pleased Grace, because it meant that Emilia was already stepping away from the baby, that she was ready to let go, that she would not cry like one young woman Grace had had who had caused such a scene that she had to be sedated. Grace held the baby and, for the first time since she started this, she began to sob. It embarrassed her to cry in front of her staff and in front of Emilia, who looked uncomfortable to see her so vulnerable. Grace thought of Emilia, years from now, wondering about this baby she was giving up.

Grace wished Emilia would change her mind. The new mother for whom the baby was meant – a woman who sold lace in Lagos – would be waiting for the call to come and collect her child, but this baby was not really hers, Grace thought. She swallowed the tears, calmed down and said brightly, 'You did well, Emilia. Try to rest now.' She handed the baby over to a nurse to clean and feed, then went to her office to call the client. The woman had been married for years without a child. Her husband's family assumed she was responsible, even though she and her husband had visited several doctors who had found nothing wrong with her. 'They could not understand why I couldn't conceive.' Her husband stopped sleeping with her and married a younger woman, sure to fill his house with children. 'Some woman his mother had found for him. What did I care? I was glad that he'd left me alone, had stopped dragging me to doctors to peer inside me with their tools and look confused when nothing appeared to be wrong.' Two years later, the new wife left. If their husband could not get two women pregnant, maybe the fault was his? She could not stay with a man whose penis was useless at firing shots. As the woman told this to Grace in her office, she doubled over in laughter. Her husband had bribed the woman to lie about why she left, 'but you can't cover the silence of an empty house. Even his mother, who'd been cruel to me, his sisters, everyone started treating me like an egg. I could do no wrong.' She guffawed. 'They praised my silence, my saintliness. If they could, they would have canonized me!' She let out a long laugh that filled the room. 'I don't care but it matters to them and it matters to him to have a baby, so here we are.'

Most people wanted sons but luckily, this woman didn't want to know. 'Whatever God gives us, we'll take. A beggar has no choice, abi? Frankly, I am over wanting a child, but I still want to stay married. I don't have the courage of my co-wife. She's young. She can marry again.

Who wants these old breasts of mine?' She wasn't old (forty-five wasn't old in today's world, Grace wanted to tell her) and she wasn't exactly a beggar. Grace had charged her a premium, a bit more than she charged others, because she wanted Emilia to have a fatter purse than she'd usually pay the *wombs*. She wanted Emilia to be able to stick it to her mechanic boyfriend and to her parents. And the woman could afford it. Women like her didn't mind paying for the comfort of doing business in a clinic that had longevity and looked like Grace's, unlike the others that were always springing up and being shut down just as quickly, because the owners didn't have enough money to bribe the police and city officials. And where they did stay open, they were often in a seedy part of town. Grace's clinic was a sprawling bungalow in the middle of a large compound surrounded by high walls. People who came were often shocked at how well kept, how *foreign* it looked, how it seemed like they'd left the chaos of Uwani behind as soon as they walked in. Here, no one heard the horns, the insults impatient drivers shouted at each other, the hawkers selling groundnut and banana and chanting *buy sweet, sweet orange*. It was a different world, fully air-conditioned with a generator that made sure that the clinic always had power (and none of those noisy things that littered the city and gave Grace a headache). Here, the generator – which was one of the more recent additions – was quiet in its efficiency. All these things had been enough to satisfy Grace. Now she couldn't wait to leave the clinic, to go home, even though Okika was still not back and the girls had not called her once. When she slept, Grace saw the faces of the pregnant women who had left their babies behind, heard their voices turn accusing, although they always left grateful for the chance they were getting to live a life unencumbered by a child they could not keep, untethered to responsibilities to an infant.

One day, Ifeatu suggested that perhaps she should visit her parents again, see her mother, forgive the woman. Grace shook her head. She couldn't, wouldn't, forgive the woman who had so spectacularly ruined her life. Ifeatu had been with her for about a week by then, going to work from Grace's and staying in to eat dinner with her because Grace did not want to go out. 'If your daughters, either of them, got pregnant now, what would you do?' Ifeatu asked Grace. She steepled her hands under her chin and looked at Grace across the table.

'God forbid ooo, but if they get pregnant, I'll keep the child. I'll raise the child. That child would be my grandchild.'

Ifeatu repeated the question as if her friend had not said anything.

'But I've said already . . .' Grace began. Ifeatu raised one hand in the air to stop her. 'Gracie, this is me you're talking to. We are in Naija ooo. Your girls are fourteen? Fifteen? They come in now and one of them tells you she's pregnant. You'll do what?'

Grace thought about it, called the scenario forth in her mind, imagined Mmuodum or Kaikele coming with that news. She'd want a termination. A child now would mess up her girl's life. She'd kill the man responsible. She'd be so angry and so hurt and so disappointed. Even thinking about it got her so agitated, she reached into her bag for a cigarette.

'I didn't know you smoked,' Ifeatu said.

'Used to. Occasionally,' Grace mumbled and put the cigarette back in her bag. Her hands shook. What must her friend think of her now, with all the secrets. Even people who knew her before Ifeatu did not know she smoked. It was something she'd hidden, smoking only inside her house. So eager had she been to cultivate a life that would not link her to her past that it had taken her until she was secure in Okika's relationship to tell him that she used to smoke. Smoking was for loose girls. For prostitutes and home wreckers. It was the lesson every girl was taught. Good girls from good homes did not smoke. Boys could smoke but they hid it from their parents, smoking only in public when they were with fellow rebellious mates. Grace had picked up smoking in nursing school out of curiosity, but also because she wanted to do something that would hurt her parents as much as they had hurt her should they ever find out. She used to imagine them hearing from someone that their daughter smoked. It'd kill them, Grace thought with every drag. But she never had the guts to let anyone catch her smoking. And then she had begun to enjoy it, the way it relaxed her after a long day, smoke circling her head like a warm hand. Still, it hadn't been difficult for her to give it up. It had been a relief to have a reason not to harm her lungs and to live with someone who kept her on her toes. Now, she was back to smoking and it was her mother's fault. All of it.

'You need to free your mother,' Ifeatu said. Grace was grateful that Ifeatu had not shown any anger or shock at any of the revelations which to her must seem like a betrayal. She hadn't asked, as Okika had, 'Do I know you at all?' And she had not walked out on her. She had sat still, in Grace's sitting room, on a Saturday afternoon while Grace unloaded her history. She had not recoiled in shock when Grace mentioned the abandoned baby or told Grace how she could have done things differently. But she had also not nodded in approval when Grace blamed her mother. She had asked the same questions in different forms. 'What would you do if Mmuodum or Kaikele came in right now and said they were pregnant?' She had asked until Grace began to see that she was not that much different from her mother, that they were affected by the same society, the same rules that she, Grace, thought she had been breaking.

Grace told Ifeatu what she would do, speaking through clenched teeth.

'And if you forced them to terminate the pregnancy while they wanted to keep the child, and they walked out and they pretended you were dead, told you they wanted nothing to do with you, what would you do?'

If they did that, Grace would seek them out. She would find them and throw herself at their feet and beg for forgiveness. If she knew where Okika and the twins were, she would go right now and beg them to come home. That they wanted nothing to do with her seemed like a death. It was crushing her. But her mother had not asked for her forgiveness, she told Ifeatu.

'Why do you think she came?' Ifeatu asked, her eyebrows shooting up, her head tilted like Princess Diana's in that old interview that TV stations still played.

'She came to tell me that Ben's parents wanted my forgiveness.'

Ifeatu let out a short, impatient grunt. Grace knew what it meant. Ifeatu knew, as Grace did, that Nigerian women of her mother's generation did not come out and say *sorry, forgive me*. They asked for it in other ways. Once, when she was in elementary school, her mother had beaten her for breaking a plate. The plate, porcelain with the illustration of a flamingo in its centre, had been a gift from an old mentor. Her mother did not even use it. Instead, it was propped on a chest, against a wall in the parlour. The young Grace would spend hours gazing at it. She was never to touch it. But one day, the temptation to run her hands over the flamingo had been so great that she reached out and picked it up. Maybe it was the excitement of holding it, but the plate slipped and shattered almost as soon as Grace had it in her hands. After her mother beat her, the woman appeared to have regretted it because she came looking for Grace minutes later, bringing her daughter two pieces of meat from the lunch she had been cooking. No one ever ate two pieces of meat in the house except Grace's father. And certainly not before the meal.

Grace stood up. She knew what she had to do.

PART TWO

One

Trans-Ekulu, Enugu

2020

Grace drummed her hand on the lip of the table as her father sat opposite her, as frail as he had looked weeks ago when she had come for the first time. He was wearing a black T-shirt. The sight of him, his narrow shoulders with the blades pointed and sharp, and his head which looked too heavy for his neck, again put Grace in mind of the poem about the vulture. She felt guilty and she tried to think of something else. The house smelled of bleach and Dettol. It was like being in a hospital. In her clinic, she counterbalanced the antiseptic smell with that of her favourite air freshener, sandalwood, which she plugged into sockets in every room. The silence stretched between them as they waited for Grace's mother to return from the market. Ifeatu had convinced Grace to go back, to see her parents again, give them another chance. Ifeatu and the pain in Grace's heart at the loss of her own children had convinced her, and so here she was watching her father silently look at her as if he wanted to drink her in. She knew that if she didn't say anything, he would sit in the silence.

'How are you doing, Daddy?' she said. The word still sounded foreign to her. Even in her mind, when she thought of her father, she never called him Daddy and yet, here she was, regressing to her childhood.

'Better than I was yesterday, worse than I'd be tomorrow. We thank God.' That too was new: a father that prefaced or ended every statement with 'God willing' or 'We thank God'. When had he become this religious? This willing to leave everything to God? Grace tried not to feel upset that when she'd had her baby, her father hadn't been willing to let God handle it. If he had, she would not have spent the past twenty-six years wondering what had become of her firstborn child, the flesh of her flesh.

The anger did not help, Ifeatu had told her. Nor did the *what ifs*. 'What's happened has happened. The question is how long are you going to hold on to the anger – and for what?'

Grace thought she could hear the rattle of her father's lungs. 'The doctors can't do anything for you?' she asked.

'They say to wait it out. No one knows what to do about this disease. Tufia!'

The bleach which suffused the house burned her eyes and she rubbed them.

'Your mother caught it and it was as if she had nothing. Lucky, if he caught it, we noticed nothing of it and neither did he. And yet here I am, months later.' He wheezed.

'Ndo.'

They were bathed in silence, neither willing to puncture it. Grace had come because Ifeatu had convinced her, but she had no idea how to go about dispensing forgiveness. Did one just come out with it? Say, 'I forgive you?' But the forgiveness had not even been sought, not asked for.

In the hour and a half she had been sitting with her father, waiting for her mother to return, he hadn't said a single word about Baby. He had been happy to see her, looking surprised when he'd opened the door to her. They had hugged, stiffly, less comfortably than they had the first time Grace came. Even in the joy on his face, Grace thought she could spy a film of wariness coating it like fine dust. She wondered if he thought she would disappear again.

'Where is . . . Lucky?' she asked, pausing to remember his name. He was at school. Grace raised her eyebrows. Schools were closed. At least, all of the public ones were.

'He goes to a private school not far from here,' her father said. 'All the money you send us, month after month. It's too much for us.'

'So you send your house boy to a private school?'

Grace hated that she felt jealous of this little boy for having the best of her parents. He lived with them in the kind of house she used to dream of living in as a child, and now they were spending money sending him to a private school as if Trans-Ekulu didn't have a public school. They were indulging him in the kind of excesses that she could never have imagined.

As if her father could hear her thoughts, he said, 'The school here is no good. Teachers using their classrooms to trade because they aren't being paid.'

Grace knew all the arguments against public schools. They were nothing like when she was young. Her own children were in a private school because of that, and she would send them to a private university. Still, her parents were spending a lot of money to train a child that wasn't theirs. And her own child? The grandchild they'd made her give away?

'I have to leave,' she said, standing up. This whole forgiveness thing? She couldn't do it. She wasn't ready. It was easy for Ifeatu to tell her to forgive. Forget. Move on. Ifeatu did not have to carry the burden her parents had foisted on her as a child. Ifeatu with her childhood spent in London. Ifeatu who talked about fighting with her parents over getting a piercing at eighteen as if it was a normal thing to do to argue with your parents, laying down your facts to counter theirs, having them listen and eventually having your way. Ifeatu who had the childhood that Grace would have liked to have, had she known it existed. Of course, Ifeatu would think forgiveness was an easy thing to do. 'They are your family,' Ifeatu said, her British accent slipping out like it did when she wasn't paying enough attention to conceal it. 'The anger at one's family never reaches the bone.'

'Wait,' her father said. 'I have something for you. Biko. Chelu. Let your mother return.' He craned his neck as if that would hasten his wife's return. The confusion on his face was replaced by something else that Grace could not immediately decipher. She could walk away now. Something told her that if she did, her parents would keep away as they had in the past. They would not come looking for her. Her father asking her to wait was his attempt to keep her from shutting the door forever.

Two

Trans-Ekulu, Enugu

2020

Grace did not trust herself to stand. She regretted not leaving when she said she would. Her legs felt so brittle she did not believe they could carry the weight of her. If she stood, she feared they would crumble and spread in a powder all over the floor. Years ago, she had taken the twins on holiday to Belgium and they'd gone to Oostende where sand sculptures of all of their favourite cartoon characters had dazzled them. Kaikele had stood in front of a Mickey Mouse statue, sitting with its legs crossed, and she asked her mother, 'If he stands up, will his legs dissolve?' Grace felt as if her legs were made of sand and that if she took any step, they would crumble.

She was still sitting when Lucky returned from school, striding in with the aggressive steps of a child entering their own home. The front door escaped him as he tried to close it and it slammed shut instead. Grace remembered that the few times in her childhood when they had had someone else living with them – a cousin, a poorer relative's child whom kinship prevented from being referred to as a house boy or house girl – they did not walk in as if Grace's parents' home was theirs too. Smart and shiny in his uniform of red and blue, white socks up to his knees and brown covered sandals, Lucky could pass for the well-loved child of any middle-class family. He did not look like anyone's servant.

House helps were scrawny like poster children for refugee camps in countries where food was scarce. Ifeatu told her once of her aunt's help who grew so fat on extra food she swiped from the kitchen that she purred like a kitten when she was asked to sweep the house, so Ifeatu's aunty began locking up food and giving the girl only one meal a day until her ribs were visible again. They had ashy legs and went to night school when all the work they had to do in the house was done. Their arms, from what Grace remembered of the Obianos' house boy – their neighbours when she was growing up – were scarred from multiple whippings for not being fast enough with their chores, for disappearing like the Obianos did to play football with other neighbourhood kids when they should have been sweeping, fetching and carrying. Doing chores that multiplied as soon as one was done. And especially if they were orphans like Lucky, brought to the township by an uncle who couldn't look after him, who wouldn't want to rock the steady roof under his head, they were treated worse than dirt. They did not carry a leather backpack full of books that had been bought for them for school. And they did not hope to go on to university (UNEC or ESUT) to become a doctor. If they did, they could not realistically expect it to come true in the way that Lucky did, answering her questions about his future with aplomb, with the confidence of someone who knew that there were resources at his disposal to make his dreams come true. Even though Grace was jealous of this boy, she was grudgingly proud of her parents for treating him as their own child. For presenting this glittering, well-fed, round-faced boy to the world as their domestic help. A child that had the freedom to dream.

'Daddy, my teacher said to tell you that the field trip has been postponed,' Lucky said. Grace watched as her father's face mirrored the boy's disappointed one. 'There will be other trips,' Grace's father said, and then to Grace, he began to explain that Lucky's class was supposed to go to some fish farm, and that the boy had been looking forward to it. Grace tuned him out. Through the windows, yellow mussaenda flowers gazed at her. Yes, she was happy that her parents treated Lucky well, but Lucky staking his claim on her family when she had no idea where Baby had ended up was too much for her to bear. She couldn't stand to be there any longer. Rage and jealousy stirred a whirlwind inside her. If she didn't go, she might say something she would regret. She stood up to leave. Her father had stopped talking, and Lucky had disappeared into one of the rooms.

'Please. There's something you have to see. I was waiting for your mother to come, but . . .' He held out a hand as if to stop her from leaving, and shouted for Lucky. Grace felt foolish for letting her parents' relationship with Lucky get to her. She hadn't needed them in a long time. She'd see what he wanted to give her, and she'd leave and never come back. She heard a door open and close, and Lucky came running in as though he'd been waiting to be called.

'Daddy?'

'Get me the newspaper lying on the drawer closest to Mommy's side of the bed.'

Grace felt a familiar stirring inside her. Lucky knew her parents so intimately as to know on which side of the bed they slept. She had to keep her emotions in check. She inhaled. Exhaled. Lucky reappeared with a newspaper and her father opened to a page with a huge asterisk at the top of it and asked her to read the highlighted words. Neon orange against the black of the print. A child looking for a mother who had left her at the corner of a quiet road in 1994. There was a phone number to call and an email address if that was preferred. She opened her mouth to ask her father if this could be Baby, but words failed her. She wanted to run out into the front yard, to wail, but no part of her body worked. It was as if the words she read were a tractor going over her body and leaving her with a wreck instead of joints that moved and vocal cords that produced sound. She had read somewhere about cloth dolls whose heads were filled with balls of wool. She felt like one of those dolls now. She was still staring at the paper, unable to look away or make sense of what she had read, when her mother opened the door and came in.

Three

Trans-Ekulu, Enugu

2020

Grace's mother's return shifted something in the room and suddenly Grace found that she had the strength to look away from the paper, to push it back to her father, to say, 'This all seems too convenient.'

Okika would have said that God worked in mysterious ways and Grace shouldn't discount its veracity just because it seemed impossible, but Okika was not here and she had no idea where he was with her twins, punishing her for something that happened years before they met. Okika could go to hell, she thought. Him and his sanctimonious self. What did he know about standing in her shoes, let alone walking in them? What did he know about life hitting you with such force that could keep you down forever if you were not attentive? She wanted to hurl things. If Okika ever came back, she would tell him that she'd never really loved him, not the way he thought she did. She would tell him that he had merely been convenient, that she didn't need him, and he could crawl back to where he had come from where everyone was a holy angel never putting a foot wrong, just waiting to get their haloes. Let him go and lick his wounds far away from her, what did she care? As long as he returned her girls to her.

God! How she missed her daughters. She missed hearing them talk about their day, asking her to buy them this and that. Asking if this or that friend could spend the night. Missed hearing their laughter. Once Okika brought back the twins, he could disappear. She was independent, she was young, she was attractive. Love and companionship weren't limited commodities heaped on trays in the market. She could always find someone else. Okika was not the only man in Enugu. He wasn't special. He didn't have two heads. The more she railed against Okika in her mind, the more the image of him flitted before her. Smiling as if he was inside her mind and could hear her, mocking her with that smile. She wanted to swat the grin off his face, and so dredged up more ways in which he wasn't special. Her mother was asking her something, so Grace dragged her mind back to the present.

'Why would anyone lie about this, eh? Maka gini?' her mother asked, slipping off her sandals and dragging out a chair to sit beside Grace. The fruit and vegetables she had bought in the market peeked out from polythene bags she had hastily thrown on the table. She called Lucky to wash them and put them away.

'How is your husband?' she asked Grace. 'And the children?' Grace mumbled something her mother did not catch, so she asked her again.

'They are gone,' Grace said, standing up now. 'You know why they are gone, Mother?' Her voice rose. She could hear Lucky stop the tap in the kitchen. He was probably listening, the nosy little usurper, but she did not care. 'They are gone because you turned up. What did you think would happen?'

Her mother closed her eyes as if she'd been blinded by lightning. Pain flashed across her face and it gave Grace some comfort. Good, she thought. Let her mother suffer as she had suffered. 'He took them and left because you dragged the past into my home. I asked you to stay away. I gave you . . . I provide for you, and all I asked for was a chance to start again, but you could not . . . would not let me!' Grace could feel her hands shaking, her heart like a fist beating in her chest, but she could not stop the words. Her father said nothing. He had his hand on the paper and did not move it.

'All I wanted was a normal life. I built that life. I worked for it. I deserved it, but you could not leave me well alone! Mba! And now . . .' She snatched the paper from under her father's hand and waved it in front of her mother, pages falling out of the paper and scattering on the floor. 'And now you give me this? What am I supposed to do with this?' She stopped to catch her breath. In that moment of exhaling, a thought marched into her mind.

'Did you do this?' She knew even as she asked that it was a ridiculous notion that her parents would try to trick her by planting this appeal in the papers, posing as her long-lost daughter, but how else to explain it? It could not be Baby. Coincidences like this did not happen, not even in Nollywood films. How was it that the minute her mother turned up, Baby turned up too? What were the chances? But why would her parents orchestrate this? It did not make sense, but she was struggling to find something else that did.

'You think we did this?' her mother said and began laughing. A loud cackle that filled the house. She stopped to wipe tears of laughter from her eyes. 'Grace, nwa m, we may be a lot of things, but your father and I are not into 419. We are not scammers. Why don't you at least call the number? We haven't because we were hoping you'd come again.' Her mother's laughter had subsided, her voice was soft, moistened by something Grace would not face yet. She looked at her father, at his face like a put-upon saint, and she knew that they had come upon the appeal the same way they came upon news about her in the newspapers that they – her father especially – obviously still read religiously. She got her news, when she did, from the radio and social media. Twitter was great for headlines. It kept her abreast of what was newsworthy and what was not. Her mother got up and squatted in front of her, surprising Grace with her agility.

'Please, call. Eh? Biko nne m. Nobody else knew of this but us, so if this person says they are who they are, maybe you should call? We did not want to be the ones to do so. It isn't our place.'

Grace thought about this. She imagined what she might say to this person who could possibly be Baby. She folded the page with the highlighted words into her purse, making sure to tuck it in well so that the paper did not snag on the zipper.

Four

New Lay Out, Enugu

2020

That night, Grace could not sleep. The hair on the back of her neck prickled as if there was a ghost in her house. Her bedroom was cold and not even sleeping under a blanket helped. She had only ever felt like this once before, back when she was a child and still believed in ghosts. Her next-door neighbour's visiting relative had died, a woman that Grace had run errands for only the day before. Grace had felt the woman's ghostly presence all day, heard her asking Grace to be a good girl and buy her a loaf of bread from the kiosk downstairs, and the hair on the back of Grace's neck had prickled so that she felt like there were ants crawling up her neck. She caught herself slapping the back of her neck several times.

There was a power outage and her generator droned all night, so that even if she had been tired, it would have been impossible for her to fall asleep. But for Okika, who thought a silent generator like the ones at the clinic were excessive, Grace would have replaced this noisy thing. There was no need to spend so much on a generator when the one they had functioned well, he said. He was always wary of living a life of luxury. He could not enjoy an expensive bottle of wine without feeling guilty about how many people the money Grace spent on it could feed. As if it was a crime to be rich and spoil oneself. What was the point, Grace asked him once, of all that hard work if they couldn't enjoy its proceeds? She didn't have to worry about what he thought now, did she? Grace brought her knees to her chest and wrapped her hands around them. She did not feel any warmer. She wanted the weight of someone else in her bed, and Ifeatu had long moved back to hers, assured that her friend would not starve herself to death. But she was getting tired of Ifeatu anyway, her friend's admonitions couched as advice. *You should forgive your parents. You should forgive this Ben. You should find Okika and make up with him, you must understand how betrayed he's feeling.* Do this. Do that. What did Ifeatu know of the pain that had been caused her?

She tossed and turned, her bed a landscape that was both unfamiliar and hostile. Since Okika left, she had been teaching herself to sleep alone again, not to miss sliding to Okika's side of the bed and being spooned by him. She had thought to herself several times that if she were white, she would have bought a dog for company, let the dog sleep in her bed like they did in oyibo films so that her bed did not seem so empty. The newspaper page she had taken from her parents lay on her chiffonier and, even in the dark, Grace could make out the crumpled ball. She had thrown it in the trash when she came home, retrieved it, crumpled it up again and thrown it away. For some reason, before going to bed, she had brought it out again and hurled it on the chiffonier across from her bed. Tomorrow, she'd throw it away. No good could come from calling the number. What were the chances that this was Baby? Coincidences like that did not happen. But the date was right, the name of the area where she dropped off her infant was correct.

> Baby abandoned in 1994. In New Haven. Seeking to find birth mother. If you're the right one get in touch with NewHavenBaby@gmail with the name of the exact street you dropped off the baby and the date. Or call 042 335182.

If her parents hadn't put out the post, then who had? Had she told Okika where she had left the baby? She did not think so – and even if she had, why would Okika want to taunt her by doing this? Whatever else he was, he was not malicious. *But he is*, a voice inside her insisted. *He took your daughters from you, so why not this too? But what if,* asked another voice that sounded suspiciously like Ifeatu's. *What if this is Baby?*
What if?
All night, the voices duelled inside her, fighting for dominance, asking her to listen to them, to burn the paper, to call the number, to light a cigarette and sleep well, to send an email. The voices tugged at her, pulling her in one direction and then another.
In the morning, before her bath, before her coffee, even as the louder of the two voices told her not to be silly, that it was too early, she picked up her phone and dialled the number. If she was going to do this, she had to do it now and she had to do it by phone. She had to hear a voice. If she heard the voice, she told herself, she would know. There was no logic to this belief, she wasn't superstitious,

but she believed it with her whole heart. The call went through. It rang a few times, and when no one picked up, Grace breathed a sigh of relief. She did not believe in miracles. Or signs. Nothing had prepared her for a life where wonders happened. Not even giving birth to her twins had converted her. She was so unlike Okika who, despite being an engineer, a dealer in science and facts, was content not to seek to understand everything. He could stand on their balcony and be lost just looking at a bird flying, reflecting not on aerodynamics but on the miracle of it. Grace, on the other hand, had a more scientific mind, yet now she took this technological failure as a sign that she was chasing after a mirage. She crumpled up the newspaper again and threw it in the trash. This time, she did not retrieve it.

Six

New Lay Out and Old GRA, Enugu

2020

Grace dithered all morning over what to wear. Should she go for casual (jeans and T-shirt); casual elegance (jeans and a button-down shirt); casual traditional (an ankara up and down)? Clothes tried and discarded gathered in a mountain in the middle of her bedroom. She had to make a good first impression, she told herself, then realized she sounded like a job applicant and laughed. What did it matter what she wore? She could not eat breakfast; her stomach was in knots and she skipped lunch as well. Besides, she could not sit still long enough to eat anything.

'Madam, anything wrong?' Cee asked as she cleared the untouched agidi and egusi soup from the table, pieces of goat meat sticking out like dunes. Meat that Grace would have demolished no matter how not hungry she was. One of her childhood fantasies that she was now living out was eating as much meat as she wanted to on any given day. It probably wasn't healthy, she agreed when Ifeatu pointed that out. 'But I ate so little meat growing up that I am still playing catch up.' It had come out as a joke, but she did mean it. Cee wasn't used to her madam leaving meat untouched. Grace said all was well, she just had no appetite.

'I'll eat it tonight. Please don't make me anything else for dinner.' The plates clattered as Cee cleared the table. Grace looked at her watch. Even accounting for traffic to Polo Park Mall on a Saturday afternoon, if she left now, she would be far too early. The clattering. Cee's eyes on her. Too much to bear. She picked up her car fob.

They had agreed to meet in a public place. Grace had arrived an hour ahead of the agreed two o'clock. Baby had arrived twenty minutes later. In recounting this first meeting, they would be unable to agree on who had seen whom first, but there was instant recognition and a long, tight embrace. Grace wasn't sure whose idea it had been or why they'd agreed to meet in a public place, but she was regretful now. All she wanted was to be on an island, alone with Baby so that she could howl, yell, sing in delight and hold her and never let go. Instead, here they were at the food court at Polo Park Mall, her tongue coated with pizza from Domino's which she couldn't taste but had ordered for something to do while waiting for Baby to turn up.

'Baby,' Grace whispered as they separated and sat. Grace thought in wonder, *just two drops of water*. Baby's eyes so huge she constantly looked surprised. Like hers. A neighbourhood child had made her cry when she was nine by calling her anya ikwikwi. Owl eyes. For a long time, she had been self-conscious about her eyes but on Baby they looked perfect. When Baby smiled to say hello, the slight gap in her teeth was the exact replica of Grace's. Then Grace's eyes settled on the nose. It was so slim she could be Fulani. Like hers. Grace noticed too the one droopy nostril like Ben's, and she felt a short, sharp stab. She had somehow forgotten that Baby had entered the world with Ben's nose. Grace stood in front of Baby, her face mask underneath her chin, and drank her in, the sight of her daughter inebriating her, dizzying her. This headiness did not make her want to sit, though. Instead, it filled her with a buoyancy that made her want to fly. She imagined that if she walked, she would bounce softly like a ball. She imagined bouncing all over the food court telling people, total strangers going about their business, that she had found Baby. Grace always thought of 'a full heart' as something of a clichéd metaphor but now she knew that it was real. She could feel the fullness of heart, so full that there was no space for anything else to find its way in. A fullness that stole her voice. She tried to talk but her words came out like a little howl, so she just stared at the young woman she still called Baby in her mind. Her real name was Onyinye. It was like looking at herself, as if she had been reincarnated in this girl she had carried in her heart all these years. O di ndu bia uwa ozo. Onyinye in an ankara jumpsuit that could have easily been Grace's (she had at least three such jumpsuits in her closet). Grace's cheekbones underneath Onyinye's sunglasses. This was bone of her bone, flesh of her flesh, blood of her blood. In the crowded mall, nothing else existed but this moment. Her heart so full, it clogged her ears so that she could no longer tell which Christmas song was blaring from the speakers, yet she had been humming along to the songs before Baby arrived.

For minutes, she just held Onyinye's hands across the table. *Flesh of my flesh. Blood of my blood.* She allowed the tears that pooled in her eyes to drop. First, she said, 'I am so sorry.' Then she asked the question the answer to which might break her heart. 'Did you . . . How was your childhood?'

Onyinye said without hesitation, as if she had expected the question, that she had had a good childhood. A splendid childhood, she said. She had one sister, Nnemka. 'Mom and Dad were great.' Her voice as hoarse as it had been on the phone. Grace didn't know if she always had this voice or if this was a temporary state. So much she didn't know. So much she wanted to know. 'We couldn't have wished for better parents,' Onyinye rasped. She hadn't known until her mother lay dying that she wasn't theirs biologically.

Grace felt both relief and jealousy. Baby had had a good life. But that life had excluded her. 'I am sorry to hear about the loss of . . . your loss.' She could not bring herself to say the word 'mother'. If Onyinye had a mother already, then what was she? *You're Baby. My baby! You have only one mother and she's right here, sitting opposite you. I am your mother.* She chided herself for her foolishness. How could she be jealous of a dead woman? A dead woman who had looked after Baby well. If she hadn't, Grace might never have had a chance to see Baby again.

Onyinye's mother, Ifesi, had died in July. 'She had COVID. We hadn't expected to lose her.' Onyinye's voice cracked. She pursed her lips, bit the inside of her lower lip and gave Grace a wan smile. 'Sorry. It's very difficult.' Grace nodded. She yearned to console Onyinye, but she had no idea how. What could she say?

'Were you two close?'

'Yes.'

Ifesi and Onyinye had been very close, so close that Onyinye, and not Nnemka or their father, had been the one sitting vigil outside the room their mother had been quarantined in until she had suddenly deteriorated and had to go into hospital. It had begun as a cough, a *hack hack hack* that interrupted Ifesi's speech. Then a fatigue that kept her in bed with muscular pains that seemed to move from one part of her body to another. No one could tell how she had got it. The house was disinfected every day. Everyone wore masks whenever they were out. There were huge bottles of hand sanitizer in every room of the house. There should have been no space for the virus to worm its way in, but it had.

Onyinye provided pills to break the fever and dull the aches, made hot soup with uda and chicken to clear her mother's nose and suppress the cough. And in a reversal of roles, she sang lullabies to her mother to lure her to sleep on the nights when sleep was far away. Love is strong but it is not the strongest of all. So many things are stronger. Illness for one. Ifesi worsened. The night she gasped out that she could not breathe, Onyinye was the only one who heard her. She called the ambulance, her heart already breaking for her mother's pain.

'We were tight. Close, like this.' She linked her pinkies together to show how tight. 'That was why I felt betrayed initially, that she didn't tell me about find . . . finding me.' She had only told Onyinye that she wasn't her biological mother the day before she died. 'It was on FaceTime because we couldn't visit her in hospital.' This mother who was so clichéd in her loving attention, all the poems and songs and lullabies about selfless mothers seemed to have been composed for her. The mother who fed her light in the dark days of her teenage years, when it seemed she was perpetually walking into a harsh harmattan haze, doubting everything. Her brains. Her beauty. Her strength.

'I had issues, you get?' She looked lost in thought, as if returning to those days. When she stopped eating because a boy she liked called her thick, asked her, 'Do you ever take a break from stuffing your face with food, Miss Fatty Fatty Bum Bum,' and waddling in front of her to imitate a walk that was nothing like how she walked, and she came home crying, her father told her not to be silly, she wasn't fat. But it was her mother who noticed how she hurt and pulled her back from that place where everything she ate was an enemy to be emptied out. In loving her, her mother led her back to loving herself. And it was this mother, whom Onyinye loved above everyone else, who hacked out the words that uprooted her life and sent her careening out of the room, banging doors, sinking into forever, shouting, 'How can I ever forgive you?' Onyinye's voice cracked and tears rolled effortlessly down her cheeks.

Grace was grateful that Onyinye felt comfortable enough with her to cry in front of her. She leaned across and wiped away her daughter's tears. Onyinye gave her another smile. 'After she told me, I was so angry with her and my father. I felt as if they'd lied to me my entire life, you get? I left the house. I didn't even want to see Nnemka. I know she didn't know, but still . . .' She stopped and took a deep breath. Grace waited for her to continue. 'I went to my best friend, Raju's. You should meet her.'

'I'd love to,' Grace said automatically, so grateful for the gift that was being proffered. Onyinye wanting her to meet her best friend. Grace didn't know what to do with her hands, trilling for joy. She put them in her lap. She remembered how she had worried before the meeting, her heart fluttering in fear and joy. Now all that worry seemed needless and she could concentrate on just the joy – although she wanted to find the boy who had made her daughter cry and make him pay.

Grace had not told anyone – not even Ifeatu, to whom she told everything these days – that she was going to see Onyinye. She had wanted to keep it to herself in case it did not work out. For all she knew, Onyinye might have been seeking her out to tell her off. She had seen that happen in an American TV drama once. An adopted child met with his biological mother only to tell her how much he hated her. 'Why could you not keep me?' the young man cried, unwilling to even listen to the birth mother he had tracked down. His adoptive parents had been abusive. 'You threw me to the wolves,' the man said. Grace had to remind herself to temper her joy and listen to her Baby.

There were days, Onyinye said, she wished her mother had never told her because she did not think she would ever be able to find the woman who gave birth to her. 'I had no idea where to begin. It seemed impossible that I'd ever . . . I did not think I'd ever find her. Find you.' Whenever she was out, she wondered if any of the women she saw was the one she was looking for. Once, at a supermarket near her house, she had felt drawn to a woman with a kente mask covering the lower part of her face. She couldn't even see what the woman looked like, but she had been sure for a second that that was her real mother. Onyinye had stopped breathing as the woman passed her by, smelling so achingly familiar. 'Of course she smelled familiar,' Onyinye said, forcing out a laugh. 'The woman was wearing the same perfume my mother had worn.' Onyinye had inherited her mother's unfinished bottle. She rationed its use, saving it for the most difficult days when the weight of her loss was too much to bear. On those days, she spritzed a little bit on her wrist and sniffed in the fullness of the Kenzo her mother had smelled of. And on another day, she'd thought the woman from whom she bought fish at Ogbete market was the one who had birthed her. She had almost asked the woman if she'd ever given birth and abandoned the baby. In Nollywood movies, the woman would have said yes, she and Onyinye would have hugged and all would have been explained and forgiven. But Ogbete was not a Nollywood set and if Onyinye had asked, she was sure the woman would have announced to the entire market that Onyinye was accusing her of secretly abandoning a baby, and others would have joined the woman to beat Onyinye to a pulp for daring to bring her insanity into the market. It was after that day that her sister had suggested a paid ad in as many dailies as possible. 'I wasn't even sure you read the papers, but my sister thought your generation – our parents' generation – probably still did. I am glad I did.'

Grace squeezed Onyinye's hand. Onyinye squeezed back. 'Baby,' she whispered. 'I am very glad you did.' They smiled at each other. That Baby was here, at the mall with her, overwhelmed Grace. How glad she was that Onyinye had been given a name that encouraged miracles, a name that put nothing above the heavens, because what was this if not a miracle? Grace was not superstitious, but she felt now that what she had heard about the potency of names in Igbo tradition had some truth to it. No power on earth could have brought Grace and Onyinye together; they were never meant to meet, so if her name hadn't precipitated it, then what had?

Onyinye wanted to hear the story of her birth and so Grace told her. She did not hold anything back. She started with Ben and ended on the night she left Baby at the corner of Okpara Square. 'Please, forgive me,' she said finally.

'You did what you had to do. You were a child. Pregnant at fifteen? Gosh! What's there to forgive?' Onyinye said and gifted her a wide smile to let her know that she wasn't just being glib. Her tears had dried, carving a trail through her carefully made-up face. 'What do you do? You look like someone I might have seen on TV?' Onyinye asked. Grace sucked in air and held it. How to be truthful without being entirely honest? She was a trained midwife, although she didn't have to do any midwifery chores she didn't want to. Grace said, 'I'm a midwife. I think I have one of those generic faces.' The first part was the truth, the second half could be true. Would Onyinye have been watching TV ten years ago at the exact time Grace's face had beamed into homes at the ribbon-cutting ceremony for the clinic? There were so many like her. Opening businesses and paying TV stations to cover the event. Would she have been able to recognize Grace from seeing her face as a guest at some of the top Enugu events? Grace doubted it. Faces blurred together unless you knew to pay attention to someone in particular. And for young people like Onyinye, the orbit in which she was a star was not on their radar. It was a mere technicality but one that gave Grace the ease of mind to tell Onyinye simply that she was a midwife making it sound like the modest role of a hired nurse, without it sounding like a lie. She hoped Onyinye wouldn't ask more probing questions. Grace did not want to have to actively lie to her. Maybe Onyinye felt the shift in the air because she did not ask Grace anything else about what she did or if she had ever been on television. She hoped Onyinye's father wouldn't immediately recognise her name. Her heart pounded. Even if he did, she reminded herself, all he'd know was that she ran a successful clinic. Unless he himself had referred someone to her, he would not know it was also a baby factory. Still she'd prefer that if Onyinye ever found out about her clinic, that she did so from Grace herself – at the right time. Ife nwelu oge. Everything has its time.

Grace would try to remember, much later, what else they talked about, but she would not remember much except that Onyinye had forgiven her and had invited her to a Christmas party she was organizing. 'My mother liked to throw parties,' Onyinye said. 'Nnemka and I are trying to keep that tradition alive. And I'd like you and . . . and my sisters if they want to, to come.' *If you can call them your sisters, why can't you call me 'Mother'*, Grace thought jealously. She was glad that Onyinye did not call her 'Aunty' as many young people called older ones. It would have been far worse than being called 'Grace' or nothing. 'Aunty' would mean that Onyinye had decided on an honorific. The way things were now, Grace could imagine that Onyinye could still call her 'Mother'.

Their goodbye hug was brief, far too brief for Grace, who felt teary. Outside the mall, a few children gathered around the carousel. Couples walked side by side, carrying shopping bags, and a young man Grace almost bumped into had a cup of ice cream. There were titters from a group of teenagers. Overhead, an eagle soared. Life was happening and, for the first time in a long while, Grace felt it surging inside her too. Apart from the birth of her twins, Grace could not imagine anything that had happened to her in her life had brought her close to this feeling. All of her body, from her toes to her hair, every single bit of her felt alive. She was sure that if she was stuck in a dark room, she would glow. *Glow-in-the-dark Grace.* All of Enugu seemed to be outside this Saturday, just a week before Christmas. Shopping. Eating. Living. Having grown up in Enugu when the mall was a park, she hated that it had become this concrete mess. But today, she loved it. It was sacred ground. It was where the Miracle of the Meeting had happened and she had held Baby in her arms again.

The radio was on in her car but she couldn't hear a word of whatever programme was on Dream FM. Her ears were full of her daughter's words. As she drove home, Enugu's roads gleaming with a new light, Onyinye's forgiveness played in a continuous loop. 'You did what you had to do, what's there to forgive?' Forgiveness so freely and so thoroughly given.

Those words propelled her to her parents' house. This time, when she said she forgave them, she would mean it. Onyinye's forgiveness had given her an uncommon strength, summoned from the core of her being, to forgive too. Whatever time was left with her parents, she wanted it to count. She would no longer look back at what might have been, because this reality was better than anything she could have imagined. And so, she could relieve herself of the burden she carried: the regrets and the anger. She could see now that the forgiving could be for her own sake, too. She would not carry Ben in her heart anymore. That he, presumably, and his family had been so haunted by the wrong that they did that they imagined there was a curse on them was enough. She amended her thoughts: it should be enough. But a gap had opened somewhere, and in that gap, she saw Ben's mother humiliated like she too had once been. She would see her, she decided. She wanted the woman to ask her for forgiveness herself, and when she gave it, she wanted her benevolence to be acknowledged in her presence. She, Grace, deserved that much.

Seven

New Haven, Enugu

2020

Grace had not bothered to make an appointment. She didn't want Ben's parents to have a chance to prepare. It was petty, she would admit this to herself, but she didn't want to give them a chance to present their best selves. If for some reason they weren't home, she would drive back to her own house and try again another day. Determined to see them, she would not give up until she did. Their house was still big, but it had lost all of the glitz and glamour it had held for her in the days when she used to sneak in with Ben. The entire house reeked of something foul, an infected wound. As Grace waited in the parlour, she felt the smell sticking on her too. That odour raked back the years, and it was 1993 again. For a minute she felt like the scared, pregnant fifteen-year-old who had come here with her mother all those years ago. She could not believe that she was about to cry. It would not do for her to cry now. She brought out a compact mirror from her bag and applied a layer of the red lipstick she always carried around. She was still wiping off red that had strayed under her bottom lip when she heard a small cough. Ben's parents had come in silently, as if they were entering not their own parlour but a church long after the service had started. Ben's mother was dressed in black, a long skirt covering her legs. She even had a black scarf on her head as if she was mourning a recently departed husband.

'Biko, who are you?' Ben's father asked. 'We weren't told who had come to visit us.' Something in his voice sounded frightened, disbelieving and knowing all at the same time. He knew, Grace realized, who she was. They were both still standing as if waiting for Grace to give them permission to sit.

'Please,' she said, gesturing to them to sit. They obeyed. Ben's father cleared his throat, but before he could say anything, Grace began. She was sorry to hear of Ben's death, but it had nothing to do with her. What had happened was in the past and she bore them no ill will. Ben's mother suddenly knelt and let out a long, mournful cry. Then she crawled over to Grace and held on to Grace's ankles.

'We are so sorry. Ndo. Biko gbaghalu.' Her grip was tighter than Grace had expected. She fought the urge to shake her ankle loose. She wished she felt sorrier for this couple who seemed so lost even in their own house, tortured by the belief that she had placed a curse on them. She wished a part of her did not take pleasure in seeing them so mightily crushed, Ben's mother kneeling at her feet, his father groaning, a man in pain. She imagined what telling them about finding Onyinye would do to them. She would not share Onyinye with these people, not even the news that she had had her, lost her and now found her. They hadn't earned that right.

Eight

New Lay Out, Enugu

2020

The next day, Grace did three things. She called Okika. When he did not pick up, she left a long message on his phone. She hoped she hadn't rambled, but the longer she thought of it, the more she thought that it did not matter. He was her husband. It felt to her as if this was the first time in all of their years together – in all of their years of being married – that she was laying herself bare to him. When she met him, she had thought it expedient to show him only the part of her that she had reinvented. She was sorry she had not trusted him with her past. She was sorry he'd found out the way he did. She should have been the one to tell him. Could he forgive her? 'Babe m,' she said. 'Please come home.' She hoped that he would play it and give her another chance. If he didn't? Then she would have to accept that it was truly over and reckon with the part she had played in rupturing their family. All those wasted years, she thought to herself, when she carried the burden of her loss alone. Okika would never have judged her for her past. She should have known that. She had been so unfair to him.

The second thing she did was to call her daughters and tell them of Onyinye. She would like them to join her at the Christmas party she had been invited to, to meet their big sister. She was sorry she had kept her a secret from them too. She should never have done so. The girls had questions. What did their sister look like? What was her name? What did she sound like? There was laughter. And tears. And then: 'We miss you too, Mommy.'

She drove to her clinic and, as she walked the corridors to her office to meet with a new client, she realized that she did not want Onyinye to ever see the clinic. There would never be the right time as long as she was in the baby-selling business. She wasn't ashamed of it, she had done a lot of good, but Grace didn't want to share this part of her life with her newly found daughter. The way Onyinye spoke of Ifesi, as if the woman was beatified, she needed to be saintly too. 'A saint and dead. You need to pull out all the works,' Ifeatu had told her when she told her friend how guilty she felt for seeing Ifesi as competition. 'I should be happy that she was a good mother, but I feel like I'd always fall short.'

'You're only human. Do what you have to do, whatever it is, no matter how difficult, to even out the competition,' Ifeatu had said. 'Let your heart lead you, not your head.'

So, the third thing that Grace did was this: she told the client that she had no baby for her. In fact, she was no longer in the business. She was closing shop. 'I'm sorry I asked you to come in today. Why don't you adopt?'

The client laughed dryly and didn't bother to answer. If she'd wanted to adopt, she told Grace, she wouldn't have come to her. She looked at Grace as if she were an alien. 'I came because I was told that babies from here are not traceable. That you make the birth certificates in the new parents' names. I came because you came highly recommended. What is it? You want more money? Name your price.' The woman sounded annoyed and impatient, her voice a cane whipping Grace.

Grace said it wasn't about the money. 'Not even for a million dollars,' she said. The woman hissed. She had wasted her time coming to Grace while she should have been somewhere else. She knocked over the bottle of hand sanitizer on Grace's desk as she stood up, snatched her expensive-looking woven bag off the table and charged out of Grace's office to find someone else who would give her what she wanted. Her type always got what they wanted; they had the money for it. It gave Grace some satisfaction to know that she could reject the money, however much it was this woman was offering to give her.

By the time Okika called her back, she could tell him that she was turning her clinic into just that: a place where women came to give birth, not to buy babies. No more side deals. She was going kosher. Vulnerable women could still have their babies there for free, but if they could not keep the babies, she would help put them in touch with an adoption agency. She never wanted to be responsible for a baby being unable to trace its birth mother. Every child deserved that. She would gather the courage to tell Felly that she wanted out of their arrangement, too. She hoped Felly would be unable to find anyone else in the business she trusted to help her separate her grandchild from its mother. Felly was discreet and had to be careful because she had a lot to lose, so there was a good chance that Grace's backing out would make it impossible for

Felly to carry out her plan. Maybe it would even force her to leave the lovers alone. Grace was happy just thinking of it. She could not make up for the past, but she could swerve away from it. Once that decision was made, a peace she had not known for a long time settled on her. It was startling because she hadn't known anything like it in a while, not since the pregnancy, not since the giving up of the baby, not since her mother turned up and threw her home into disarray. Now, she knew that her former life had had to be shaken, destroyed, for this peace, this cleansing, to emerge.

Nine

New Lay Out, Enugu

2020

A week was too long to wait, Onyinye said when she called Grace up the next day, causing Grace's heart to flutter. Did Grace want to come over during the week before the party? She wanted Grace to meet her father and her sister.

'I'd love to,' Grace said even before Onyinye had finished asking, as if she was afraid that if she didn't, the invitation would be recanted.

'I don't want them to meet you only at the party, you get?' Onyinye said.

'I understand,' Grace said.

She wanted to ask if her daughters could come, but then she thought better of it. She did not want to overwhelm the girl. And she wanted, she saw now, to have Onyinye to herself a bit longer. She wanted to see where Onyinye lived. To see the family she belonged to. They still had a lot to talk about. There was still so much about her she didn't know. Like what was her favourite food? What were her hobbies? Was she seeing someone? If Grace turned up with her twins, Onyinye's attention would be split. No, better to go on her own and let the sisters meet each other at another time. Grace felt like a child who had been invited to a birthday party. She was so eager she was buzzing with excitement. She kept looking at the clock. Onyinye had said she had errands to run but should be back by three-thirty so Grace could come after then. When Cee – who still worked weekends even though Grace had told her there was no need – asked her what she wanted for lunch at about noon, she said nothing. She couldn't get anything past her throat because excitement and nervousness had taken up every inch of her stomach. As Cee turned back to return to the kitchen, Grace called her back into the living room.

'Sit down, Cee,' she said. Cee hesitated and Grace smiled to show her she was not in trouble. Cee sat at the edge of the sofa beside Grace. It was strange seeing her sit down in the living room and Grace realized to her shame that Cee had never sat down on the sofa. She had cleaned the room but whenever she did sit down, she sat in the kitchen. This whole house, Grace thought, and the woman did not dare to use any room but the kitchen. Cee even used the bathroom in the Boys' Quarters which the gateman and the driver used. *But I never asked her not to use the rest of the house*, Grace consoled herself.

'Relax, Cee,' Grace said. 'I don't bite.'

Cee's smile was fleeting. Grace turned and held Cee's hands. She could not remember ever touching this woman who had worked for her for years, and who watched out for her. She had never sat down this close to her before. Cee smelled of clean washing although the sleeves of her patterned blouse were damp with sweat. It was an old blouse of Grace's. Occasionally, when she got tired of clothes or grew out of them, she made a bundle of them and gave them to Cee, so much smaller than Grace that she often swam in the clothes. The blouse was loose on her and the two safety pins with which Cee fastened the front where buttons were missing glinted through the holes. Cee looked down at her feet, her body facing the wall so that Grace only saw her profile.

'Cee,' Grace said. 'Please look at me. I want you to look at me when I say this. Relax.'

Cee looked up. She turned sideways so that she faced Grace.

'Thank you,' Grace said. 'For everything.' And before she could think of it, her arms reached out to Cee and hugged the woman so fiercely that Cee let out a small gasp. Grace held on as if she was trying to transfer her gratitude by osmosis. She could feel the tension in Cee's shoulders.

'If there's anything you want for Christmas, anything at all,' Grace said when she let Cee go, 'tell me.'

Cee smiled, exposing a chipped tooth Grace had never noticed, and stood up as if the show of emotion had embarrassed her. She sprinted back into the kitchen.

On the way to Onyinye's, Grace called Ifeatu. She told her she felt bad for not being better friends with Cee. 'You can't be friends with your domestics,' Ifeatu told her. 'She's not your friend. She's your employee. Just raise her salary. Throw in a super huge bonus this Christmas. If you start becoming her friend, you'll confuse the poor woman. Next thing you know, she'll start avoiding you and looking for a new job. Never mix business with pleasure. She has her friends, you have yours.'

Grace did not argue with her friend, but she thought that after all the years Cee had spent with them, after how Cee had looked after her, Grace knew so little about the woman, and it mortified her. That shame was replaced soon with a burning nervousness as she got nearer to the address Onyinye had given her. Her hands shook on the steering wheel. She could not believe her luck that not only had she found Baby, but that Baby wanted a relationship with her. Happiness swamped her, drenched her like pouring rain. Everyone should share in that joy, she thought, including Cee. By the time she parked under a mango tree by the gate to the house, she was already smiling like a Christmas goat.

Ten

Independence Lay Out, Enugu

2020

'She loved filling the house with people and food and music.' Grace nodded and smiled as Onyinye spoke of her mother, Ifesi. Grace had been there for at least an hour and their conversation had hardly strayed from Ifesi. She did not, Grace told herself, feel any envy for the relationship that Ifesi had had with Onyinye. There was a huge Christmas tree in the sitting room covered in lights and baubles and Grace had complimented it as soon as she walked in. 'Beautiful tree,' she said. That was enough for Onyinye to launch into talk of her mother. Ifesi had loved Christmas. 'If Mommy were still alive, we would have had a Christmas village complete with snow underneath that tree!' she said. 'She loved Christmas and Christmas parties.' Grace had listened and smiled and aahed. Akanna, Onyinye's father, and Nnemka, her sister, were in the living room too, chipping in with a comment here and a comment there, but it was Onyinye doing all the talking. Grace wondered if Onyinye was nervous. She hadn't been this voluble the first time they met. On a heavy wooden chest against a pale wall were photographs of Ifesi. It was easy to see, in the pictures, just how much Nnemka looked like both parents and for the first time Grace felt a sadness for Baby growing up in this family where no one looked like her. She wondered if it bothered Onyinye, but it was not something she could ask.

Christmas cards hung like lights from ribbons all over the living room. Cards with pictures of the Madonna and baby Jesus, of angels and the Three Wise Men, of a grey bearded Father Christmas carrying a sack of toys. 'We hadn't even wanted to celebrate Christmas,' Akanna said when Onyinye stopped talking. He was dressed in black, a man in mourning. His head was shaved and Grace didn't know if he was bald or if the shaving was also was part of his mourning tradition. Igbo widows were always clean shaven and wore white or black for anything from six months to a year, but she hadn't known any man do it for his wife. Widowers did not mourn so publicly; culture did not demand it of them.

Ifesi's death had left her family too spent to welcome the Christmas spirit she loved so well – and which they had loved because of her – but Onyinye had insisted. 'She is so much like her mother, this one,' Akanna said. His eyes on his eldest were tender. Grace knew then that Onyinye could never have felt out of place in this home where she was so completely loved.

'Thank you,' Grace said, looking at both Akanna and Nnemka. 'Thank you for looking after Bay . . . after Onyinye.'

'Nothing to thank,' Akanna said, waving off the thanks. His wedding band glittered on his finger.

'She has always been ours. When she came to tell me that she wanted to find you, I admit, I was slightly worried.'

He smiled at the recollection of a worry that he now knew he needn't have had. 'I asked her, "Have you ever felt that you did not belong to your mother and me? Why do you want to find this woman? Did we fail you in any way?" Now I am glad that she has you.' Grace searched for hints of accusation underneath his words but there were none. She had been nervous about meeting Onyinye's father and sister. She had wondered what they must think of her, especially Akanna. She had worried that she would be judged and found wanting, even though Onyinye had told her that they were looking forward to meeting her. She did not imagine that they would not wonder what kind of woman would abandon a new baby on a street corner.

'The only person you should care about is your child,' Ifeatu had responded when Grace told her that she felt as if she was driving to the gallows going to meet Onyinye's family. 'And the girl has forgiven you, hasn't she?' Ifeatu asked. Yet, Grace had worried walking into the house.

Akanna had embraced her like family. 'We've all had COVID,' Akanna had said. 'It's okay to hug. We are all very happy you are here.' His eyes twinkled. If he recognised Grace, he didn't say a word about it. Grace had been taken aback by the effusiveness of the welcome, but Akanna, with the sort of face that made Grace think of the word 'jovial', had put her at ease. 'You're now a member of the family as well!' he said. It touched Grace so much that tears welled up behind her eyes. Nnemka had hugged her too and to Grace's delight had remarked almost immediately, 'You two look so alike!'

Grace recalled what Onyinye had told her at their first meeting. 'If my mother hadn't told me she wasn't my biological mother, I am not sure my father would ever have done so.' She had never felt as if she did not belong, but once she knew she wasn't her parents' biological child, she felt unmoored and wanted to be rooted to someone. She needed it to quiet her restless heart. She hadn't told her father she was searching for her birth mother until after she had put the ad in the newspaper because already, she noticed, her father was unnaturally careful around her, his affections exaggerated. When he hugged Onyinye, he held her far longer than he usually did. It made her feel both guilty and uncomfortable. She could not even talk to her sister. While Nnemka seemed to understand her need to find her roots, Onyinye had told Grace, she could not shake the feeling that her sister felt that the search was a form of betrayal. And that had made her feel guilty too. But all of that seemed to be in the past now. Grace had felt the genuineness in their welcome of her.

'I am very happy she found you,' Akanna told Grace. A warmth seeped into Grace's soul. She wanted to ask, but did not dare to, if she could see pictures of Onyinye through the years. Onyinye as a baby. As a toddler, as a school girl.

Grace cracked her knuckles and Onyinye said, 'Oh my God! I do that too! Now I know where I get it from.' Grace wanted to spring up from the sofa and hold Onyinye in her arms and never have to let go. This was better than being called 'Mother'. Her heart was so full it was spilling over, and she found herself chuckling. She could not help it.

Eleven

New Lay Out, Enugu

2020

Grace was on a high, buzzing as she drove home from Independence Lay Out, wondering how it was possible that four hours had slipped by so quickly, yet so packed. How much she had learned about Onyinye. She loved okra soup; she liked dancing but wasn't a good dancer; she had postponed going to law school for one year because of her mother's death. It wasn't only because they were close, but also because she had felt so adrift after discovering the truth of her relationship to her family that she hadn't wanted to do anything.

'Nothing seemed sure anymore. Nothing seemed real.' Not even the fact that she had always wanted to be a lawyer. It was her best friend, Raju, who convinced her not to give it up completely.

'Oh, you must go to law school,' Grace told Onyinye. The twins were not interested in any of the traditional professional fields. 'I don't mind,' Grace said when Onyinye asked her if she did. 'Whatever makes them happy,' she said.

'Very unlike your typical African mother,' Onyinye said. 'Your children are lucky. My mother was like that too.'

You are my child too, Grace screamed inside.

Nnemka and Akanna left them to run some errands and Grace gathered the courage to ask if she could see old photos of Onyinye.

'Oh my God! I don't know if I want you seeing photos of me as a child!' Onyinye joked and gave a fake shudder. 'I had a phase when I liked slipping into my mother's high-heeled shoes and she made sure to take loads of photos of me in them!' She laughed and Grace dutifully laughed back although she was trying hard to suppress the jealousy that had reared its head again.

Grace listened as Onyinye recounted events from her childhood as they flipped through the photos. In all of the photos of Onyinye and Nnemka as children, they were almost always dressed alike. Up until Onyinye turned fourteen and rebelled for being too old to play *dressalike*, Ifesi had dressed her daughters up in identical clothes, fitting them in matching dresses with satin bows. Two little girls who looked nothing alike. 'Strangers were always shocked to discover we were sisters,' Onyinye said. *How come? How come? How come you're so yellow but your parents and your sister are dark? How come?* The questions, right from elementary school, making her feel always like she didn't belong, like something was missing. The questions had made her look through heaps of dusty family pictures looking for someone who looked like her. Even slightly. *So who looks like Mommy and who looks like Daddy?* Some adult asked them once at a birthday party. Nnemka had Ifesi's bow legs and Akanna's full lips. She had Ifesi's dimples and Akanna's slender fingers. The dimples could be traced back to great grandma's family – there were pictures to prove this. All of Onyinye's uncles on her father's side had the slim, slender fingers of the family. Wasted on a girl who would not wear nail polish and show them off, Ifesi would complain. *If only your sister had inherited them.* Onyinye with hands like a man's and nails that needed lots of work to tame. But once she was allowed to, she had those nails filed and manicured and painted into submission. Beautiful reds and pinks and mauves. 'See?' She showed off her beautifully manicured nails to Grace. Grace took her hands and kissed them. If she had inherited the famous family fingers, Onyinye said, she would have been shoving them into people's faces. 'No one would hear word for me, I swear.' She let out a giddy laugh. Grace thought, looking at her own hands, *But you did inherit your family's fingers. You have my hands.*

No one in the family swam. In the family's history, there were stories of drownings and near drownings, a prophet's warning about an ancestor's pact with some water spirit that would continue to take or try to take victims until its bottomless stomach was filled kept the fear alive. Nnemka could not even stand under a shower. So when Raju asked her to join her for swimming lessons, Onyinye had repeated the family lore, although she found that she was curious to try.

'But you are you and not your family. And if we took lessons together, we could go swimming at the club with my Mummy-Papa every Sunday and they'll buy us suya and meat pie and Chapman', Raju said with all the wisdom of a nine-year-old. Raju got her parents involved when Ifesi and Akanna refused to give their permission, and their arguments eventually won Ifesi and Akanna over. 'Let the girl learn. It'll be good for her. It's a good skill to have. We'll be watching her every second of the lesson,' Raju's Mummy-Papa said.

Onyinye discovered she loved water. 'Such a natural,' the instructor said, delighted to have a student who did not stand at the edge of the pool, shaking with fear. Not one she had to cajole, coerce, bribe, gently prod into the welcoming pool. 'Such a natural,' she said again when Onyinye said her family had an aversion to water. 'Are you sure they are your real family?' A joke. But how was this instructor to know that this was a question Onyinye had heard many times before. *Are you sure you and Nnemka are sisters?* Onyinye held her tears in until she went home and she unleashed them into her father's arms, who told her the instructor was just being silly and let her have an extra scoop of ice cream. 'No one looks like you because you're special, Onyinye. There is only one of you.'

Grace wanted to go back in time and console Baby. She tried not to think of the babies that she herself had placed with people and for whom she had made sure that they would never be able to find their biological parents. Guilt cascaded down her body and covered her in a blanket so thick, so dark, that for a moment, she could not hear anything else but a voice telling her that she was evil. But she wasn't evil, she said to the voice. What of all the people she had helped who couldn't have children? And all those she had helped who had the babies but couldn't keep them? That widow who got the money she needed to escape the grubby hands of her brother-in-law? The girl who could go back to school? Grace wasn't evil. She might have been doing it for the wrong reasons, but her baby factory was not evil.

Maybe it wasn't, but her misery had delighted in company. She had spent years separating babies and mothers because it made her feel better that she was not the only mother to have her baby taken from her with no hope of being reunited. How had she not seen this before now? It was so clear to her now that it had always been about not being alone in her suffering. She was no better than Doctor Hicks after all. This was what had made her ashamed. She had always waved off Okika's concerns about the ethics of what she did by reminding him of the amount of good, the joy it brought to both the babies' new families and the women who gave up their children for money. *But Grace, it was never only about that.* She could no longer lie to herself. At the mall, when she told Onyinye she was a midwife, she hadn't mentioned that she had a clinic because she did not want to let it slip that she ran a baby factory. It wasn't shame that had stopped her, and while she couldn't tell it then, she knew now that it was a recognition that what she did there was not only an act of charity.

But if Onyinye ever found out, the voice told her, it would kill their relationship. *Then I'll make sure she never does,* Grace responded to the voice, her voice intimidated by the boom of the guilt. In the darkness of that guilt, she heard Onyinye say, 'But someone does look like me.' Grace smiled back at her, the darkness replaced by the light of Baby's words. She told Grace of one woman who had responded to her ad. Saying she was Onyinye's mother and could Onyinye send her money. They both laughed. 'Times are hard,' Grace said. 'Lots of people are looking for ways to make easy cash.' Onyinye stuttered slightly, so slightly it was easy to miss, the same way Grace's father did. It seemed to Grace that she'd always known Onyinye, but was only now putting specific experiences to the person she'd always known.

At the IMT bus stop, there was a traffic jam even though the school was closed because of the pandemic, and Grace, usually impatient with traffic jams, noticed that she did not care. When a beggar rapped on her window, she took out a fistful of notes from her glove compartment without even counting them. At this moment, she could give out everything she owned and still be content. 'Merry Christmas,' she said to the beggar, a young woman with crutches, dropping the largesse into the beggar's proffered bowl. As the beggar rained blessings on her for her magnanimity, wishing her *plenty happiness, sister*, Grace thought that she had already been blessed. She was at the peak of happiness. As she turned right towards Queen's School, a Keke cut in front of Grace and she had to brake abruptly to keep from hitting him. The driver waved his apologies and Grace did not shout at him as she would have on a normal day, to ask him if he had a death wish. She smiled and waved her acceptance back. It wasn't until she got home that the full weight of this second meeting dawned on her and she locked herself in her room and cried tears of joy.

Twelve

New Lay Out, Enugu

2020

The next day, Grace rattled around her house in her bathrobe, unable to sit still. She opened and closed doors, walked the length and breadth of her house like a toy a child had wound up and left to carve its own path. Too many questions, too many thoughts were crawling inside her like ants on sugar. Sometime between falling asleep last night and waking up in the morning, doubts had begun to dance over her joy. Cee made her an omelette and boiled yam for breakfast, but she just nibbled at it, too distracted by something she couldn't name. She had not heard back from Okika since she'd left the message on his phone asking him for forgiveness. Would he ever forgive her? She couldn't keep away from her clinic forever, but she was worried that if she went in and was confronted by a pregnant woman needing help in exchange for money, she wouldn't know how to turn them away. She wouldn't have the heart to. 'When genuinely desperate people beg,' Ifeatu remarked once, 'they know how to make you give in. They snivel.' Ifeatu had been talking about an uncle of hers who had ten children but expected family to help.

No matter how much she resolved not to, the moment the uncle began to beg, listing all the ways in which life had been unfair to him, she always gave in. Making the decision to quit had been easy; it was sticking to it that Grace was worried about. She had to warn her parents and her daughters that she was going to become less generous, no more lavish allowances or expensive gifts. Without the money the baby placements brought in, could she even afford to keep the clinic? Ifeatu was right. Maybe she was being hasty. She may not have had an altruistic motive in mind when she set up the clinic, but there was no denying, was there, that she had provided a lot of good? As if to mock her, someone outside her gate let out a loud bellowing laugh. She cut off a small piece of yam and chewed on it meditatively, trying to imagine a life where she did not have to make difficult decisions, where her life had unfolded exactly as she had dreamed it would as a child. But in that world Onyinye wouldn't have existed. She shook her head to clear it. It didn't help to think like this. It was her akalaka to have Baby. She could not rewrite fate. She thought back to yesterday, to being in Onyinye's house.

The first time they met had seemed like the answer to a prayer. Yesterday was an unexpected bonus, and after yesterday, she knew that she and Onyinye could fall into the kind of relationship that she had with the twins: no awkwardness, no secrets. Or very little of it. The twins had been to the clinic, but she did not think they were au fait with all the services she provided. They had never seemed curious to know and so she had never had the need to lie to them. But Onyinye was older. She was more curious. She may ask the kind of questions

Mmuodum and Kaikele hadn't thought to ask. How could she explain her lifestyle to her daughter without revealing the truth? How many midwives could afford to live the way she did, even with a husband who had a good job? Onyinye's parents were wealthy but she, Grace, was likely wealthier. Whatever she planned to do with the clinic, she had to do it before she and Onyinye got any closer.

'You know that you have plenty of competition for maternity clinics? Pregnant women are spoiled for choice!' Ifeatu told her when she heard. But could Ifeatu not see, Grace asked, that not everything was about money? She knew she sounded self-righteous, like the sort of people she and Ifeatu sometimes ridiculed. Pastors on TV who spoke of the limits of wealth to grant happiness when everyone knew that money could open many doors. Grace had always thought that the more money she had, the happier she would be, but it could not have been happiness because she always felt the hole that Baby left in her heart. But Grace understood now what it meant to be willing to sacrifice wealth for peace of mind. Except now she wasn't sure that she could actually do it. How would she fill her days if she were to lose the clinic? She couldn't go back to working for someone else. She had money in the bank but, like Ifeatu reminded her, money in the bank doesn't last forever. And if Okika never came back, she would need, more than ever, to have a steady income. Why hadn't she thought to invest? To diversify? She sighed. She was just like Nigeria and oil, she thought. All her eggs in one basket, and now that basket was precariously balanced at the edge of a bench, about to topple over. She pushed the plate of yam away and called for Cee to clear the table.

Thirteen

New Lay Out, Enugu

2020

Grace wanted to know, she had to know, what singular stroke of fortune had led Akanna and Ifesi to Onyinye. She had tried not to imagine of how differently this could have turned out. Her baby could have been picked up by a family of molesters. After all, there had been no one to screen the family she went to. That she had gone to a family that raised her as one of theirs, that loved her as if she were their own from the day she was found, was a miracle. If all of the babies Grace placed went to families where they were loved like Onyinye was, then she had done well. She told herself that the reason why she insisted on giving them to families with means and who were desperate for children was because she hoped they would be well looked after, even though she never thought of the babies again once they left her clinic. It hadn't been because she didn't care, she said to herself. Then why? She didn't dare to pursue the thought. She had recently read a story in the *Vanguard* about a woman in Uyo whose boyfriend sold her baby for N300,000 against her will. The woman hadn't even known. She was doing love-love with a man who tricked her into trading their three-day-old baby to a visitor – he'd said he 'just wanted to carry the baby'. The boyfriend had given her N25,000 and kicked her out. The girl spat fire but it didn't burn him and she was in the papers begging Nigerians for help with finding her baby. Anyone who could part with N300,000 in this economy wasn't going to be easy to find, and so Grace knew that the woman had most likely lost that baby for good. Grace hadn't tricked anyone and shouldn't feel the heat of the woman's fire on her neck remembering the story now. She said a little prayer, but she was not sure if it was for forgiveness or for gratitude.

She called Akanna. 'I just wanted to say thank you for everything,' she said, working up the courage to ask the questions she wanted to ask. Akanna said no, *they* were grateful. Onyinye was every parent's dream. He paused and Grace jumped in before she lost her nerve and asked more about that night. 'We'd been married eighteen months,' he said. 'Onyinye came at a very fortuitous time.' Ifesi had been worried about not being able to have a baby.

Eighteen months was not long enough to worry, the doctors had said, but worry they did. Or Ifesi did. It was easier for Akanna not to, Ifesi said when he told her she was worrying too much. It wasn't his body people were waiting to see change, to engorge itself and prove that it belonged to a woman. So, the doctors' assurances did little to allay Ifesi's worry. Grace could imagine that not having a child was easier on Akanna than it was on Ifesi. No one ever called a man barren. How often did pastors ask for 'women wanting children' to come to the altar to be blessed? Women. Never men. How often were childless men referred to as 'that man who hasn't given birth yet'?

Childlessness became the identifier of women in marriages with no children to show for it. The woman from whom she sometimes bought wholesale detergent was known in Ogbete as nwanyi afu na-aka amuro nwa. That woman who hasn't given birth yet. Her husband who sometimes came to the store was known as the husband of nwanyi afu na-aka amuro nwa. Grace saw the desperation and the relief in the faces of her female clientele. So yes, she understood Ifesi's impatience.

One doctor the couple saw had even tested Akanna too and congratulated him on the virility of his soldiers. If his soldiers were virile, why were they all shooting blanks, Ifesi wanted to know and no one could tell her. 'My mother wasn't disturbing us but Ifesi's was on her case. Every day it was, "Why are you not pregnant yet?" That was the mantra Ifesi heard every time she saw the woman. Her mother already had grandchildren, so it wasn't as if anyone was robbing her of becoming a grandmother. "You know that's not why I am asking," her mother said. The worry eating up her insides spilling out all over her words.'

Ifesi's mother was the third wife of a man whose first two wives had been unable to give birth. Although Ifesi's mother was younger in age and stature to the two wives, she got preferential treatment. After her husband died, the other two wives were sent out of the home by Ifesi's father's family. There was nothing tying them to the homestead, no children to root them in place. Whenever Ifesi's mother told the story – and she did often to Ifesi and her siblings – it was with both gratitude to the fate that kept her from destitution by granting her children and a sadness for her co-wives whose only crime had been their inability to have children. 'You must have children, you girls, or you're only one foot in your husbands' homes.' Ifesi had often wondered how far her pious mother, head of the St Sebastian's Anglican Women's choir, would have been prepared to go to make sure she escaped the fate of her co-wives. It seemed odd to her adult self that a man who was unable to have children with two women would go on to sire multiple ones with a third. When she worried, it wasn't that Akanna's family would kick her out should, God forbid, Akanna die. They owned what little property they had together. All the titles and deeds were in both their names. Times had changed since her mother's time, even though now and then she heard stories of men dying and their wives discovering that they'd willed their property to some lovechild the women had never heard of. Akanna would never do that to her, even if they didn't co-own everything. He loved her too much to break her like that. When she worried, it was because she was eager to have a child with Akanna. Something that two of them made. She had also always assumed, in all their years of careful sex, that once she was ready to have a baby and stopped taking precautions, she would very easily get pregnant. And yet here they were, a year and a half into legal, unprotected, loving sex and her womb was still as empty as it had always been. She could not bear the thought of never having a child especially as people she knew were getting pregnant and having babies as easily as if they were sneezing. Even her own younger sister, who got married the year after she did, was pregnant. Every time Ifesi saw her, she complained of swollen ankles and stretch marks. 'I'd take your swollen ankles and stretch marks, any day,' Ifesi told her, which shut her sister up but not for very long. Ifesi wanted all the inconveniences of pregnancy, strangers telling her what to eat and what to avoid, asking when the baby was due, for the chance of holding her own child. She dutifully ate the yam her mother made with agbon – coconut – leaves, but neither the yam nor the coconut leaves moved her womb into compliance.

'It's not a competition,' Akanna said when Ifesi pointed out to him everyone they knew popping babies. She pointed out babies every time they went out, and these babies were everywhere. So when, on the night of Akanna's birthday, they had gone out for a meal and drinks, and had taken a long walk on a deserted street, and Ifesi said, 'It's a baby!' Akanna had thought she had conjured one up from her imagination. But in that basket, like Moses a long time ago, was indeed a baby. They did not think before they grabbed it. It was only when they got home, only after they'd checked that it was a real live baby, that they started to wonder what to do about it. The stump of her umbilical cord was still attached. She had a head full of fine, dark hair. There was no hospital band around her wrist. There was no note. No compass to locate the woman who had birthed her. 'She was just this star, shining bright on a lonely road, so we took her.'

For Ifesi, it was simple. They would keep the baby. 'I did not see how we could keep someone else's child.' They argued back and forth, their voices rising like dust and settling on the house.

'How are we going to keep a child we don't know the parents of?'

'What do you suggest we do? Drop her off where we found her?'

'No, call the police. Take her to the police station.'

'Where do you think we are? Abroad?' Ifesi asked.

But they had gone to the police station the next day. They'd fed the baby, cleaned the baby and gone to the station at Thinkers Corner on Abakaliki Road to say they'd found a baby and to ask if any baby had been reported missing. The policeman they spoke to asked them for money to buy a pen to take down their statement, paper to write it on and then threatened to charge them with child abduction if they did not pay him to 'make the case go away'. On the way back from the station, the baby now somewhat legally theirs, Ifesi began to laugh.

'You let me go to that station on purpose?' Akanna asked.

Ifesi nodded and spurted out between laughs, 'I had to let you see for yourself that it was a ridiculous idea.' Akanna pouted, lifted one hand off the steering wheel to touch the bundle Ifesi was cradling and began to laugh too.

They had told very few people of the arrival, mostly only family. But they hadn't even told them the full truth. They'd said they'd found the baby dumped outside their door with a note asking them to look after her. The person who left the note had also written that they knew Akanna and Ifesi well, that the baby had no one else in the world and that God would bless them for taking the baby. 'Just like manna from heaven,' Ifesi's mother said in Akanna's presence, her voice flat enough to suggest that she did not entirely believe the story. Later, she cornered Ifesi alone in the backyard and asked her for the truth. While Ifesi was still weighing whether or not to confess all to her mother, the woman said, 'She's your husband's, is she not? He got another woman pregnant?'

Ifesi began to say something, the thought of her husband cheating on her and springing another woman's baby on her so unimaginably ridiculous that she wanted to laugh, but she thought better of it. She swallowed the 'no' rising up her throat. It was the better option, she knew, to have her mother think that the baby was Akanna's than to find out the truth. If her mother thought the baby had traceable bloodline, she would accept the baby as a grandchild more easily. 'As long as he's just going to other women for babies and coming home to you, you're safe. Satisfy him in all the ways he asks, or you'll end up sleeping with a plantain to satisfy yourself!'

One day, four months after the baby — whom they named Onyinye for the gift that she was — was spirited into their lives, Ifesi turned to Akanna in bed and said simply, 'I am pregnant,' her face radiant. 'I feel it like a warmth in my stomach.' They had just finished making love, slipped in while the baby slept. Akanna was skeptical but said nothing. After almost two years of not being able to conceive, to suddenly do so seemed unlikely. But he had gone out and bought not one, but two test kits, both of which confirmed what Ifesi already knew. Later, her gynaecologist would tell her it was because she had stopped worrying about whether or not she could get pregnant. Ifesi tut-tutted. She knew better. It wasn't the lack of stress, it was Onyinye, the baby they'd brought home and loved, that reached into the world where only babies could and begged a sibling for herself. Everyone knew that.

Her mother said it was all the herbs she concocted for

her. 'I used extra coconut leaves the last time I made yam for you.' Ifesi let her take the credit. She didn't care. A child with a full stomach doesn't concern itself with who made the food that's filled it.

Grace listened and marvelled at the love that still soaked Akanna's voice when he spoke about his wife. This was the family her baby had gone to. Had she been to handpick a family herself, she was sure she couldn't have done better.

Fourteen

Uwani, Enugu

2020

Grace's mother-in-law used to say that anything worth doing was worth doing immediately. There was no sense dragging it out. Procrastination, she said, was for those who were not convinced they were doing the right thing. For those waiting to have their mind changed. She had repeated it often as she, impatient and sullen with Grace for not letting her be a proper mother to her, packed up and went back to her own house in Mgbwo. Grace regretted now that her own fears had stopped her from having a good relationship — or any relationship at all for that matter — with a woman with whom she could have got along. When Grace thought of the woman now, it was with a tender ache in her heart, and it was usually always to recall something Okika's mother had said. She was right, Grace thought, about procrastinating. She had spent all night weighing it in her mind and she knew that no matter how difficult, no matter the sacrifice, she had to do the right thing. And she had to do it immediately.

There was a moment when Grace saw the panic on the faces of her nurses and doctors when she almost changed her mind, but that moment passed. She would have to let everyone go. Once the final patients were dispensed with, she was closing down. Better to make a complete break so that there was never a chance of her being tempted. She would sell everything, open another business. Maybe a private school. Or a day care centre. She wasn't sure yet. It was only the old doctor, emboldened by his age, who asked her why. He was making good money with her, more money than he had made in all his years of working at a government hospital. He had just bought his oldest grandchild a Jeep as a wedding gift. 'Why are you suddenly quitting?' His eyes bored into Grace's. Challenging her. 'Personal reasons,' Grace said. 'Please clear your desks immediately.' She walked out before she could change her mind, before the look on the recently graduated doctor's face crumpled even more, before they all tore into her. She did not know that she had the strength to carry their disappointments on her shoulders. Did they think this was easy for her to do? Owning the clinic was a dream of hers and she was very proud of the success she had made of it. But when she looked deep into her heart, when she dared to, she saw an image of herself that she could no longer accommodate.

Ifeatu had told her not to be hasty, but how could she not be? She thought that her friend was being too hard on herself. 'You're helping vulnerable women, what's wrong with it?'

'I am exploiting them, that's what.'

'So what are the options for these women? To throw their babies away like you were forced to?' Could Ifeatu not see, Grace asked, that she could not be party to any child not being able to trace their birth parents? Ifeatu did not understand. 'And what of the loss of income?' Did she know how many private schools and day care centres there were? Was she aware that her savings would not last forever? These were real fears, but Grace was ready to face them. 'I can't change your mind, can I?' Ifeatu said, her voice flat so that Grace knew she wasn't even asking a question. She knew that Grace's mind was made up. 'I'll support you ooo, but if you ask me, this isn't the right decision.'

Grace had Ifeatu's voice in her head now, but soon hers was replaced by the words and image of the mad man in Ogbete market who sometimes loitered near where Grace bought wholesale detergent. He was always chanting 'Forward, forward ever, backward, backward never. Full throttle, no reversing' as he mimicked a car driving, raising dust. Grace hardly ever paid him any attention, holding her nose against the stench of the market – the mounds of dirt and the pungent odour of urine – and rushing as she always was to the clean smell of detergent, but his words pushed aside Ifeatu's and gave Grace some resolve. Everyone would have to adjust. Even Grace herself. Okika earned enough working for a private firm to keep them comfortable, but the business-class flights to London and Dubai a few times a year would have to stop. And was that a bad thing? That her children would lead normal lives? That she would cut down on her own excesses? Finding Onyinye and being able to be truthful about what she did was worth it. And whatever was worth doing was worth doing right now.

Later, she would regret not sending in security guards to make sure things did not go missing – boxes of noodles and tins of milk and cartons of vitamin tablets and paracetamol tablets which she stocked in the clinic warehouse so that the women who were responsible for the babies she placed were well nourished. Even the painting she had liked of a pregnant woman hanging in the hallway was gone by the time she had hired a truck to remove what she could from the building.

Fifteen

New Lay Out, Enugu

2020

Okika called on the Wednesday before Christmas, *Babe m* flashing like a beam of light on the screen of her phone. Grace held on to the door of the refrigerator she had just opened, forgetting whether or not she had been reaching for a yogurt or the chin-chin she liked to cool, and just stared at the phone on the kitchen counter beside the fridge. The cold air from the fridge blasted her face but she stood still for a minute, immobile, turned to a rock of salt like Lot's wife, unable to think. It stopped ringing and then began again. She reached for it at the same time as she slammed the fridge door closed. She grabbed the phone, wedging it between her ear and her shoulder. 'Hello?' Her breath quickened to hear his voice, but he sounded tired, quieter than normal, and her heart, which had soared at *Babe m* on her screen, drooped and dropped. Whatever it was he was calling her for, it could not be good news. Whatever it was would devastate her. She closed the fridge door and walked on jelly legs to the sitting room so that Cee, who was pounding crayfish for lunch, would not witness her total unspooling. She paced the sitting room as she asked him how the twins were. He began to say something and stopped. She could hear a loud guffaw in the background and the sound of something breaking. 'I'll be right there,' he shouted to someone and said 'hello' again to Grace as if he had only just called.

'Hello,' Grace echoed. 'How are umu ejima m?' He wouldn't answer when she asked again how the girls were. And when she tried to sound casual and interested and asked, 'Any plans for Christmas?' he barely let her finish before cutting in to ask if she was home the next day. He wanted to come for a chat. 'What time is good for you?' He sounded so formal that Grace knew this was the end.

She walked around with the phone in her hand and stopped in front of an enlarged photo of Okika, the twins and herself on the wall between the guest toilet and the dining room. This was her favourite photo of them, taken at some wedding by one of those wedding photographers that hounded guests with unsolicited photos of themselves taken and printed within the hour. Grace hadn't even noticed the photograph being taken, even though she had been looking at the general direction of the camera. Okika's chin was tilted as if he was pointing out something. Mmuodum was showing her sister something she had cupped in her hand. Grace liked the way all four of them looked sitting around the circular plastic table at the reception. Relaxed and happy, complete pieces of a puzzle. Strangers were always telling her how beautiful the girls were, how they wished they too were twins or had twins and if she (and Okika) could tell the girls apart. They could, although the girls, once they were old enough to enjoy it, fooled their friends and teachers. But how could they tell such identical twins apart, the more insistent strangers asked. 'The heart always knows,' Grace always answered. It wasn't true, though. Kaikele blinked a little more rapidly than Mmuodum did, and no matter how much they tried to fool their parents, they never succeeded. Grace's heart hurt thinking of it.

'Grace? What time?'

'Anytime,' she said. He was probably coming to formalize the break, to tell her that he wanted a divorce. 'I'll be home the whole day.' Resigned to her fate, she suddenly wanted to get it out of the way and so she said, 'In the morning. As early as you can make it.' She didn't get a chance to ask about the twins again before he hung up.

The next morning, Grace hadn't even got into the scented bath she was running when Cee let out a loud squeal that shook the house and barrelled Grace quickly out of the bathroom to see what the fuss was about. Okika and her twins were at the door. The girls with long matching braids as if they had dressed up for an important visit. Okika looked pleased with himself and a scintilla of hope rose in Grace's chest and began a jig there. If he was here with the twins, maybe he had come home? At first, she just stood looking at her husband and her twins, thinking, 'This is all mine.' And then they were all hugging and Grace was crying. The girls had questions about their new sister. And how soon could they see her? And their grandparents? When could they meet? Grace laughed and said soon to both, but she and their father had to talk. Okika held her and said, 'We couldn't stay away. I have missed you so, so much.' Then he held her face and kissed her. 'You asked me to come home, and here I am.'

'So all I had to do was ask?' she teased.

Soon, the house shifted into its normal contours and the sound of music blasting from one of the twins' rooms filtered to Okika and Grace in their own room, making up for all the months they were apart in words and in deed. Okika held Grace, and she felt like someone who had been in the desert for so long and was now drawing water. The morning sun slanted into her room and spilled into the room like something precious and Grace wished she could catch the rays in her fist. She wanted always to remember this, always to imagine that everything – even this much happiness – would always be possible.

Sixteen

Emene, Enugu

2020

The DNA test was a formality, Onyinye said, but the TV station had demanded it. She had sent in the story of the happy reunion to *Families!* It was a new reality show that fashioned itself after an American TV show full of explosive family revelations and happy endings. Grace wasn't one for reality TV, but Onyinye gobbled them up. All the foreign ones – Oprah and Jerry Springer and Judge Judy and the new ones taking over Enugu's airwaves. So, Onyinye had sent in their story and within weeks, a producer had sent her an enthusiastic response, inviting them to the show. And offering to put her in touch with a ghostwriter to write the story of Onyinye and Grace's reunion. People would love it. The book would do well. They could make a documentary of it. There were all these possibilities, but they needed scientific proof. The show would pay for a DNA test, taken at a doctor's office where they'd send the newly reunited mother and daughter. And Onyinye had been desperate to go on the show. Their story could encourage someone else to find their birth family. It could expose her to a Nollywood director who would give her a role in a film. No one who saw them together could doubt that they were related, but the producers of the programme were adamant they could not come on the show unless they had DNA proof. Two weeks after the party, Onyinye and Grace, in identical jeans and T-shirts completely by accident, were in a doctor's practice in Emene where the TV station had sent them to be swabbed and pricked for proof of their relationship.

The doctor was a jovial, small woman who talked the entire time. 'Any fool can see that you are related,' she said as she explained why she had to do both a buccal swab and draw blood. 'Often, one is enough, but these people like to be thorough. There, we are all done.' She'd send off the samples to the lab; the results would be sent to the station and a copy to them as well, and she was looking forward to watching their show on TV. The results should be ready within ten days. 'Keep an eye out for a DHL mail because we all know that our post office doesn't work.' She laughed and waved off their thanks.

Grace hadn't spent her days waiting for the letter, and when it arrived, she hadn't torn it open all giddy from excitement. Her delight came from Onyinye's own delight. The test wouldn't tell her anything she didn't know already; it wouldn't make any difference to the relationship she already had with her daughter. She had planned a celebration of science's validation of what had already been proven, but Onyinye wanted to make a ceremony of it. They'd open it up together at Grace's, surrounded by family. Then, they'd have a celebratory dinner with her sister and father at Genesis. All week, Onyinye hadn't stopped talking of it, and her delight infected Grace so that by the time the envelope arrived, she herself was also looking forward to all the pomp around opening it.

Onyinye arrived at the house within an hour of the envelope arriving at hers, a gift bag in her hands. Grace's had arrived earlier in the day, and she had waited for Onyinye to come. In the gift bag was a bag, the same brown bag Onyinye had. 'We could both carry our matching bags to *Families!*' she said. Grace thanked her and set the bag down on the dining table, around which everyone sat. The twins and Okika counted down from ten to zero as instructed by Onyinye, and then she and her mother tore open their envelopes and brought out the test results. Grace was still looking at hers, trying to make sense of it, when Onyinye let out a shriek, stood from her chair and bolted out through the door. Everything happened, it seemed to Grace, as if in slow motion. Okika running after Onyinye, the twins crowding their mother, something heavy pressing into her chest until she too let out a scream so loud that she was sure it shook the walls of the house. She could not tell, if anyone asked, how she made it from the table to the bedroom. Or when.

Seventeen

New Lay Out, Enugu

2020

Grace walked as if underwater, barely able to breathe, all the days blurring into one like a huge messy drawing. She stayed in bed for days. Longer? Months? She did not know. All she knew was that she was aware of the twins coming into her room to try to get her to eat. Okika bringing her food to eat. Everything she ate tasting like sawdust. Then finally, one day, her mother striding into her room, carrying a tray of food. Who had asked her to come?

'Okika told me what happened. How is Onyinye dealing with it?' Grace had no answer. She'd barely had energy to think of Onyinye. She understood why they told you on planes that in case of emergency, to get your oxygen mask on first before helping secure someone else's. How could she think of Onyinye when she herself was so broken? Her mother kept talking, not giving her a chance to respond. She told Grace of the little boy who lived with them. Of how she had cried the day the boy was so ill he couldn't stand up. 'When I thought that I could lose him, I cried like I would cry if he had come out of my own womb. That boy is my son. Does it matter that we don't share blood? Where it matters is here.' She placed a hand on her chest. 'He feels like a son in here. So, where does it feel like Onyinye is yours?' Grace did not answer. Instead, she sat up in bed, leaned across to her mother and hugged her. Then she began to cry. With each tear, the tightness in her chest loosened a bit more. 'All I know,' her mother said, 'is that you've found my grandchild.'

When Grace called Onyinye, it was not with the hope that the relationship could be rekindled. It was not with any kind of hope. Okika, ever practical, had warned her against dangerous optimism, no matter what her mother said. So, when Onyinye agreed to meet, it was all more than Grace could bear. If she saw Onyinye, if the girl saw her, something might be salvaged from the damage the DNA result had wrought.

Eighteen

New Lay Out and Independence Lay Out, Enugu

2020

Cee brought the letter in to Grace while she was painting her nails. Inside the DHL bag was a letter from the same hospital where she and Onyinye had gone for the DNA tests. Grace's heart skipped a beat. Why would they send her the same test result twice? Was it a mistake? It seemed like a bad omen, on this day that she and Onyinye were meeting. A reminder that, no matter what her mother said, no matter what she felt in her heart, Onyinye was not Baby; that Baby was still somewhere out in the world – or worse, dead. As she reached out to take the letter from Cee, she knocked over the bottle of polish. The trail of red it left looked like bloody tears on her vanity table, making its way to the bag that Onyinye had bought her for the TV show. Bad omen, she said to herself again. 'Where did you get this from?' Her voice was a squeak. Don't be silly, she told herself. There was no need to be superstitious now. Cee said a courier had brought it. Grace withdrew her hand, and asked Cee to leave it on her bed instead. She would not open it because she already knew what it was. She would not touch it lest it brought her bad luck. So what if she was superstitious? She would open the letter later, but not before seeing Onyinye.

They had agreed to meet at the same venue as their first meeting, Grace choosing it because she believed in signs. If they met there, she convinced herself, then the meeting would go well. She had intended to carry the bag from Onyinye, something to remind her that, for a while at least, she had believed that they were biological mother and daughter. Maybe they could find their way back there. No matter what Okika said, Grace knew that in her heart, Onyinye felt like her daughter, and like her mother said, that had to count for something. That the intense love she felt for Onyinye when she thought she was Baby was still there, and that it had nothing to do with blood. Grace blew on her nails to dry the polish quicker. She was still blowing when her phone began to ring, Onyinye's name flashing across the screen. Her heart stopped. What if Onyinye was calling to cancel the meeting? First the letter, now Onyinye calling. She inhaled. Picked up her phone. 'Hello?'

Later, much later, the letter open before her and Onyinye beside her, Grace would think that as much as she wanted to strangle someone at the lab for mixing up their kits, as much as she wanted to sue the DNA testing company for the weeks of needless torture they had given her for their unforgivable 'human error', that her life was beautiful.

When Onyinye next held a party at her house, Grace and her family, including her parents, were the earliest guests to arrive. Grace wondered if she was overdressed in her matching skirt suit. Maybe she should have followed her twins' lead and worn jeans. 'You look beautiful,' Okika assured her. The twins hugged Onyinye, and then began immediately to talk about all the ways in which they looked alike.

'I always wanted a big sister,' Mmuodum said, and Kaikele nodded. 'And now we get two, just like that!' Mmuodum said as Nnemka joined them. Grace's heart swelled. She had to pry Onyinye away from the twins to get her to meet Okika and her grandparents properly.

'May the eyes with which I see you not kill me,' Grace's father said, and, overcome with emotion, he began to sob. He removed the matching cloth cap on his head to wipe his eyes. To Grace's shock, he knelt in front of Onyinye and began to ask for forgiveness. Onyinye looked embarrassed, unsure of what to do. Then she knelt down. Grace joined them and soon they were all holding hands on the floor, sobbing until they began to laugh at something one of them said. In Grace's favourite picture of the day, which she hung up on the wall between the guest toilet and the dining room, Onyinye sat between Grace and Okika, Mmuodum and Kaikele on either side of their parents, Akanna beside Mmuodum and Nnemka beside Kaikele. With one hand each on Onyinye's and Nnemka's shoulders were Grace's parents. The smile on everyone's face was so easy – the sort of smile, Grace would say, that filled a stomach like food.

Acknowledgements

To God, for the gift of writing – this talent that has brought me joy and opened the world to me – I say thank you. Chukwu Okike, dalu. Without writing, my world would be poorer.

I am grateful to my readers. Without you, my writing would seem like an exercise in futility – like one shouting in a cell, isolated from everyone else.

To my agent, Kate Johnson of Wolf Literary Agency, I thank you for being my guide on this journey, for steering me through the waters.

To Ellah Wakatama and Michelle Dotter, I am deeply thankful for the way you grasp my vision, for always asking the right questions to ensure the story grows as it should, that the tree is limned from the forest. Thanks for believing in my writing, and for taking a chance on me.

To Rali Chorbadzhiyska and Brodie McKenzie, editorial assistants who worked on *Grace*, and to Vicki Rutherford, also at Canongate – thank you for your invaluable service.

To everyone who read the early drafts and offered comments – you know yourselves – I hope the final product is one you are proud of.

To my mom and dad (enjoying your pride never gets

old), thank you for investing in your children, for telling us that we could, for always making us believe in the validity of our dreams. I don't know that I would have pursued writing if you had clipped my wings.

To my siblings, Jane, Winnie, Maureen, Nnamdi, Okey, and Blessing – if I could handpick siblings, I'd choose you all over and over again. Udo. Thank you for always beating my drum.

To my sons, thank you for being my cheerleaders, for the hugs, the games, the fun. I will not always be the mother you want, but I promise to always be the mother that you need. And please, pick up your phone when I call (you know who you are ☺).

To Dani, for your enthusiasm in my writing – thank you. Welcome to the family, daughter.

And finally, to my husband, love of my youth, bringer of bottomless coffees, Papa of Stefaan, Ralueke, Tomike, and Jefeechi, Ogbuefi Jan – I bless the day you walked into my dorm at UNN. How we've grown in the years since! May we have many, many more years together.